Always
YOU

Always YOU

a Falling for You Romance

LUCINDA WHITNEY

Lange House Press

Cover design ©2019 Lange House Press
Layout and Formatting by LJP Creative
Published by Lange House Press

First Printing April 2019

ISBN-10: 1-944137-44-1
ISBN-13: 978-1-944137-44-1

CHAPTER ONE

*W*hat was so magical about a letter from Elliot that she could hardly wait to read it?

Isabel Antunes passed a hand over the pocket of her blazer. She'd been biding her time all day, going through her duties as director of the academy while the paper rustled against the satin lining of the pocket. But the opportunity never came, not even at lunch. Instead, she'd had to solve a minor crisis in the absence of the chairman.

She walked out of the iron gates and the security guy closed them behind her. She turned to look at the familiar building, gray stone and red roof tiles ablaze in the late summer sun, and its clean lines and large square windows blending in with the Lisbon neighborhood of squat apartment buildings and tree-lined streets. The air was still warm and she took a deep breath. The last bell had rung forty-five minutes before, and she was finally leaving. If anything else came up, it would have to wait until Monday.

She shifted her crossbody bag and looked around. Cristina was supposed to have waited for her but was nowhere to be seen. She had probably stopped to chat with the lady who worked at the newspaper stand. Again. Isabel started up the street, treading carefully to avoid catching her high heels on the spaces between the black and white cobblestones. The sidewalks of Lisbon were renowned worldwide but should have come with intermittent warnings about wearing sensible shoes. She knew better, but once or twice a month her shoe weakness over-ruled her sensible side. Unfortunately, when it came to fashion and regret, her memory was usually short. Soon enough she'd make the same mistake again.

At the intersection, Isabel stopped by the cross-walk. Friday's early evening traffic buzzed past her and she took a step back behind the other people waiting to cross. She reached in her pocket and drew out the envelope, her gaze lingering over the block letters that spelled her name. A small smile tugged at her mouth. He still mixed upper case letters with lowercase ones, just as he had in high school.

The light changed to green and Isabel stepped forward with the others as they moved to cross the street.

"Isabel. Stop." Cristina's voice reached Isabel from behind the crowd.

Isabel turned and craned her neck to find Cristina.

From the corner of her eye, a large object barreled toward her. A jolt of pain caught her left side and a body slammed into her shoulder, hurtling her backward against the pavement. Her teeth rattled, snagging her lower lip. She squeezed her eyes shut. Screams and a whoosh of breath rang too close to her.

For a moment, there was nothing else but the act of breathing.

In. Out. In. Out.

She lay flat on the hard surface, her eyes still closed. The smell of rubber and asphalt competed with another scent, something closer and more pleasant.

"Are you all right?" a male voice said near to her. A deep, rich voice. Someone she didn't know. Someone who spoke English. Not Portuguese.

A hand touched her forehead and the hairs on her arm rose. The touch was firm, almost with a sense of urgency. Another hand slipped something soft behind her neck. Slowly, other sensations returned to her: the heaviness in her limbs, the dull throb on her head, the light pressure of fingers against her cheek. It was a comforting gesture, and Isabel exhaled with relief.

"Let me through. I'm her friend!" That voice she knew. Cristina.

The warm touch withdrew and someone gripped her hand. Long, strong fingers. Another hand touched her side at the hip. She winced. It hurt there too.

"Isabel, can you hear me?"

Isabel opened her eyes. Two faces looked down on her, one with straight brown hair in a side braid, another framed with red hair and freckled skin. Lots of pale, brown freckles. And a pair of warm, green eyes, filled with concern.

The freckled man helped her sit up slowly. He kept her hand in his until she was stable. Isabel studied the place where his fingers met hers. Even his knuckles had freckles. She raised her eyes to him and his expression softened. His hair stuck up in all directions, a mass of unruly, thick red strands the color of oak leaves at the tail end of autumn. The strange thought stopped her. She must have hit her head hard to be comparing a man to the colors of the season.

Cristina grabbed Isabel's hand away from his. "Just sit here for a minute. Don't try to stand up."

Isabel did as she was told. Sharpness had taken over her body and breathing wasn't easy.

At the sound of a siren, the small crowd of onlookers shifted. After a moment, they parted, and a paramedic came through, kneeling on the asphalt. He shined a light in Isabel's eyes and asked her stupid questions she wouldn't want to answer under normal circumstances, much less after falling on the street in broad daylight at the busiest time of day.

Had it been just a fall? Not too far from where she sat, a bicycle lay on its side, straddling the sidewalk and street. The chain had come off and some of the spokes were bent.

The paramedic grabbed her chin. "Look this way, please."

Isabel protested his ministrations but it didn't matter. Apparently, hitting her head on the pavement stripped her of good sense and free agency, and she was unable to persuade anyone that she retained her normal mental capacity. They ignored her reassurances and strapped her onto a gurney.

The red-haired man stepped into her field of view. He stretched out a hand and wrapped his fingers around Isabel's wrist, then turned to the paramedics. "Where are you taking her? What's the name of the hospital?"

If anything, the look of concern had deepened. Why did he look so worried? Were her injuries more serious than she thought?

His voice grew insistent. "Please, you need to tell me where she's going."

As the paramedics loaded her into the back of the ambulance, he took a step to follow her, but someone held him back.

"You've helped enough already," Cristina said in a tight voice. "I'm the one going with her, not you."

The paramedics took Isabel to the emergency room for a long wait before she would be able to have an X-ray. Aside from a goose egg on the back of her head, she had a cut on her lip, scratches on her hands, and bruises on her forearms. She was probably bruised in other parts she couldn't see but didn't have a concussion, which was good. When they finally released her, Cristina called a taxi to take Isabel home.

Isabel exited slowly when the taxi arrived in front of her apartment building. Unfortunately, her body had caught up after the adrenaline surge from the fall, and the soreness in her muscles bothered her with the smallest of movements, even mounting a few steps to the lobby where the elevator awaited.

Cristina took the keys from Isabel and opened the door to her apartment. "Are you sure you don't want me to call anyone?" She flipped the light switch.

Isabel shuffled to the living room and sank on the sofa. "No, I'll be all right." She took a breath and touched her temples. There was no one to call who could come. "I'll just take a shower and rest."

Cristina sat across from her. "Maybe you should leave the door open, in case you need some help."

Isabel looked down at herself. Her pantyhose were torn and her blouse had grease stains on the wrists. Maybe the dry cleaners could do something for it. "I won't be long." She rose slowly.

Cristina stood as well, her arms raised as if ready to catch Isabel. "Okay, you go do that, and I'll fix some tea."

Once in her bedroom, Isabel eyed her bed. As much as she wanted to crawl in it and forget about the past few hours, she padded to the en suite bathroom and changed out of her battered clothes.

After a quick, careful shower Isabel put on her pajamas, piled the pillows against the headboard, and sat, closing her eyes. Her body screamed in protest in more places than she could identify. The soreness was spreading at an alarming speed.

Cristina entered the bedroom carrying a tray. "No falling asleep yet. I've got lemon balm tea and toast, with a side of painkillers." She placed it on the nightstand and then sat at the edge of the bed. "For both of us. I need some calming down too."

Isabel reached for the cup with one hand and the medicine with the other. "Thanks, Cristina." She blew on the pale, gold liquid before swallowing the pills. "For this and for bringing me home. I hope you didn't miss anything important."

Cristina waved her hand. "Not much. I texted Mando and told him we'll meet tomorrow instead." She took her own cup and brought it to her lips.

"Was he okay with that?" Isabel sipped.

Cristina nodded. "He's probably at the café with his friends, and we'll have all day tomorrow." She lowered the cup. "How do you feel?"

Isabel exhaled. "Like I was run down by a garbage truck."

"Just a man on a bike. I saw him coming around the corner but I didn't reach you in time." She shook her head. "It was scary. He wasn't going really fast, but you were looking down."

Isabel sat up and winced. "My letter. I was looking down at my letter."

"What letter?"

"I was holding it. I hope I didn't lose it." Isabel grabbed the sheets, but Cristina held out a hand to stop her.

"You stay there. I'll go find it." Cristina rose from the bed and walked to the living room. "It's probably in the plastic bag the hospital sent home with you."

She returned with the bag in hand and sat by Isabel. "They put everything inside the bag, but I didn't go through it."

Isabel reached for it. As long as she found the letter, she didn't care. Hands trembling, she rifled through the contents. There was no envelope. Her heart jumped. No, this couldn't be. She reached for the blazer and slipped her fingers inside the pocket. Trying not to panic, she moved to the other pocket and almost laughed in relief when she touched the paper. "It's here," she said, her voice strangely breathless.

Cristina sat back at the edge of the bed. "That must be some letter."

"From a friend." Isabel resisted the urge to smooth the paper and set the envelope down on her lap instead.

Cristina waggled her eyebrows. "A special friend, I'm guessing. You've been holding out on me," she said in a teasing voice.

Isabel smiled. "Yes, he's special, but not in that way." She paused. "You'll laugh if I tell you."

Cristina crossed her legs and leaned forward. "I promise I won't. Now I'm curious."

Isabel breathed in, then started. "Did your English teachers ever arrange pen pals for your class?"

"Yes, in eighth grade. I got some girl in California, if I remember, but it didn't last long."

Isabel stroked the familiar postage stamp with the

effigy of the British queen. "My teacher assigned us the pen pals in the ninth grade. She had a teacher friend in England and they swapped classes. Then she told us we had to write to the student whose name we drew for the rest of the school year, and that we could write anything we wanted." She paused. She'd written that first letter three times before sending it. "I got a boy named Elliot. The first thing he wrote was that Elliot was a pen name, not his real name, because his father didn't want him to exchange real information."

Cristina's eyes widened. "You mean to say—"

Isabel held up the letter in her hand. "We wrote for the whole school year and through the summer. Remember that historical cartoon series, Amélie and the Duke of Gransville? I used the name Amélie as my pen name. At the start of tenth grade, we decided to continue writing and agreed to exchange post office box addresses since we didn't have the same teachers anymore."

"And you've never stopped writing?"

"We slowed down a bit at the start of university." It had taken almost a year to resume their correspondence. "When we started up again, we agreed to keep the personal information out of it. No expectations and no demands."

Cristina shook her head. "Then what do you two write about?"

"Anything really. About books and movies and the places we go. As long as we don't share details that could identify us, we can write about it."

"That is crazy, Isabel." Cristina looked at the envelope. "And you don't even know his real name or what he looks like or how old he is?"

Isabel shook her head. "I know he's my age, since we were in the same grade, and that he lives in London." She paused. "Well, he mails his letters from London."

"And he knows you live in Lisbon."

Isabel nodded. "I mail my letters from the central post office and that's all he knows about me." He also knew the one movie she watched over and over, how much she'd agonized over which degree to study in university, and her favorite garden in Lisbon when she needed time to herself. He liked getting up early to watch the sunrise, volunteering at the local shelter once a month, and he'd read all the Sherlock Holmes books during the summer before eleventh grade.

Cristina gestured at the letter. "And this is why you didn't see the biker."

Isabel closed her eyes and shards of memory flashed through her mind. "He had gentle eyes."

"The biker? I hardly noticed what he looked like until he pulled off his helmet." She raised her hands and waved them around her head. "Then all this red hair tumbled out. I didn't notice his eyes. He was acting very agitated and tried to get in the ambulance with you. He kept saying he couldn't leave you."

"Really?" Isabel sat up. "What did you tell him?"

"I told him he'd done enough already. But then a policeman held him back. For a red-haired guy, he was pretty good looking. And I'm not very keen on redheads."

Isabel raised an eyebrow.

"My first boyfriend was a redhead and a cheater," Cristina said.

Isabel nodded, not knowing how to respond to that. Her thoughts turned to the man on the bike, his concerned look, and the way he had held her hand. Although they had shared just a few moments between them, she could still feel the gentle touch of his fingers lending her a sense of calm. "I think he was American."

"You might be right, now that I think about it. I was paying more attention to you than him."

Cristina rose and took the tray to the kitchen. She returned a few moments later. "I'll leave now. You look ready to fall asleep." She lowered her voice. "I hope you can get some rest." She stood from the bed and walked to the door. "At least we don't have to be at the academy till Monday morning."

"Amen to that." Isabel exhaled in relief. She'd have the whole weekend to recover.

After Cristina left, Isabel retrieved the letter opener from the drawer in the nightstand and slit the envelope. She took a deep, steadying breath. It had been almost a month since Elliot's last letter. Her heart skipped a beat at the sight of the familiar handwriting, angular and slanted to the left.

She ignored her heart. Elliot was a pen pal, nothing more.

CHAPTER TWO

Dear Amélie,

I finally did it! You're always saying we should be brave and it's about time I was. I got a new job doing something completely different from what I've been doing until now. Surprise! Yeah, I even surprised myself.

I know, I know. The "rules." No particulars and no details. Just know that it involves a big change for me, and you know how I feel about change.

As I was looking for a suitcase, I came across a box full of letters from when we started writing each other. My dad must have shoved it in the closet when he brought some stuff over last time he was here. I can't believe it's been so long! I wrote some really dumb things when I was in secondary school, that's for sure. Thanks for not telling me at the time. ;)

Well, my faithful friend, I'll be reverting to emails for a while, like I did a few years back when I was out of the country (maybe one day I'll tell you more about it). I got a new email address though: elliotbestpenpal@mail.com. Wish me lots of luck!
Your best pen pal,
Elliot

൏

To: elliotbestpenpal@mail.com
From: ameliefaithfulfriend@mail.com

Dear Elliot,

You are indeed my best pen pal, if not by content at least by default since all my other pen pals stopped writing me years and years ago (someone has to keep you humble).

I have a similar box full of letters in my bedroom closet. Hard to believe it's been almost fifteen years since we started our correspondence. I still remember my English teacher drawing the names in 9th grade. Just our luck we got paired. I never noticed that you wrote dumb things. You must have been writing those to someone else.

Congratulations on your big change! I'm so excited for you! I will live vicariously through you, even if we don't exchange details. I'm still at the same job and I don't have the courage to change. I must confess, I liked it a lot better a few years ago when I first started, and sometimes I wonder if I'm making a difference in the lives of those around me, like I had intended to. One day at a time, like Grandmother used to say.

Emails will be fine. We are in the 21st century after all. I know your big change will keep you busy, but this is the address you can write when you find yourself with a free moment.

Your faithful friend,
Amélie

P.S.—I knew you were out of the country for a while. You let it slip a time or two, but I was too much of a lady to mention it. :)

CHAPTER THREE

Simon entered the apartment and locked the door behind him. He dragged himself to the sofa and let the messenger bag slip to the floor. He exhaled slowly, placed his elbows on his knees and rested his forehead against his palms.

That moment when he approached the young woman down on the pavement, Simon's world had stopped—she'd had the envelope, the one he had sent Amélie the day before leaving London.

How was that possible? How could it be that the young woman he'd crashed into was the same one he'd been writing for years?

What a day.

It had started out well but crashing into a pedestrian at a busy intersection during rush hour had not been part of his plans. He'd tried stopping but hadn't been able to slow in time. The young woman had been distracted and didn't see him until it was too late. The impact had slammed her hard, her bag and a piece of paper she'd been holding flying from her grasp. His stomach clenched, still sick with worry at the image of the her lying on the pavement. He couldn't get the memory out of his mind.

He shook his head and stood, trying to make sense of what had happened.

In the few minutes while they'd waited for the paramedics to come, Simon had stayed beside her, wishing he could do more but not knowing what. Holding her hand had calmed him, and he'd kept her fingers in his. Then he'd slipped the letter into the pocket of her blazer, not able to deal with the discovery he'd just made when her wellbeing was more important.

Simon had tried to find out which hospital they'd taken her to, but nobody would tell him anything. In a country where so many spoke English all the time, it was just his luck not to find anyone who did when he needed it most. The young woman who'd claimed to be her friend had spoken English but she had been extremely protective and had tried to keep him at a distance from the injured young woman. In his preoccupation to stay beside her, he'd probably come off as slightly imbalanced. He couldn't blame her for shielding her friend.

When a uniformed policeman arrived at the scene to take his statement, he kept Simon for several minutes. The officer's English had not been very good, but after talking to a few witnesses, he'd appeared to be satisfied and had sent Simon on his way. By then, Simon had lost all chance of following the ambulance.

What a day, indeed.

He went through the small apartment and flicked the lights on. After a long shower and changing into jeans and a t-shirt, he peeked inside the refrigerator. One Greek yogurt and some bottled water. Nothing else had magically appeared since morning. Take-out for dinner again.

How many times had he second-guessed his decision to move to Lisbon? He couldn't speak Portuguese, not anything beyond obrigado and bom dia, and there was only so much he could do with thank you and good morning. Thanks to the translation app on his smartphone and the great number of natives who spoke English, he was doing all right so far. But he'd only been in the city for a few days, and that wasn't enough to make an educated prediction for the rest of this stay.

He was not an impulsive man; quite the opposite. Decisions came after a lot of thought and introspection, and he always weighed all the pros and cons of every choice. Life-altering decisions, like moving to another country, required added pondering and even meditation, of which he had done plenty. The prevailing feeling had always been the same: a calm and tender peace. And now here he was, doing something so out of character with his nature that doubts crept up almost on a daily basis.

His father had questioned his true motives, even though he knew the real reason behind Simon's decision. Simon had steered all conversation away from the topic effectively squashing any discussion about it. Taking this job in Lisbon was something he had to do and that was the end of it. In any case, it was too late to go back, both geographically and professionally. He had signed a contract with The British Academy in Lisbon and he was committed for one term.

He looked through his wallet before leaving, making sure he had enough small bills to pay for the food. Once on the street, Simon paused and ran a hand through his hair. The evening was clear and warm and the sounds and lights of the city filtered out to him. There was a different vitality in Lisbon, something always going on, not so unlike London, but with its own atmosphere and flavor. In a way, it was familiar to him, not only the city but his perspective on it.

A perspective which was not his own, of course. How many times had he read Amélie's letters and her account of day trips and favorite places in Lisbon? How many times had he thought of coming over and spending the day with her at those same places?

Maybe he was crazy, looking for a young woman whose real name he didn't even know. But the idea of finding out who she was had been gnawing at him for over a year, growing a little more with each letter, until he couldn't ignore it any longer.

At first, he'd brushed it off, reasoning it was his approaching birthday, the big 3-0, that had him sentimental and considering something so insane. But his birthday came and went and the feeling persisted until he made a decision. After that, the peaceful feelings felt more real.

So he'd tried to discover the name of the school she attended when they first started exchanging letters, but his ninth-grade teacher had since passed away. Simon had looked through the stacks of envelopes searching for an address that wasn't a post office box and somehow those were missing as well. Dad had been quiet at first, as he brought over the boxes Simon had left behind when he left for a humanitarian trip and then university. But it wasn't too hard to guess what he was doing, was it?

How could he not try to find her? How could he pretend she wasn't his best friend?

After this afternoon's events, he couldn't shake the growing conviction that he had indeed met Amélie, if only for a few minutes. Why else would she have the letter he had written as Elliot?

Once back at the apartment, Simon pulled the small metal table into the middle of the balcony and gave it a quick wipe down. He transferred half the food to a plate and stuck the container into the refrigerator for tomorrow.

His cell phone rang, and he pushed the button. "Hey, Dad, how are you?"

"Hello, Simon. Hope I'm not interrupting anything."

The familiar voice and formality brought a smile to Simon's lips. Even after living in England for so many years, Simon had never developed a full British accent, despite his native father. People always thought it was funny how they sounded so different.

"Nope, I was just sitting down to eat something out on the balcony." Simon pushed the food around with his fork.

"I take it the weather is nice, then."

Simon looked to the city, the red tiled roofs and the light clinging to the surface of the river visible through the buildings in the waning day. Toward the center, historic landmarks and the occasional modern building shared the skyline unequally. The locals called the area the Baixa and Simon recognized its familiar pattern from pictures he'd seen before coming. "Yes, very nice. It still feels like summer. I have a good view toward the estuary and people were still out enjoying their last days of vacation earlier today."

Dad cleared his throat. "Did you go by the school yet? What do they call it?"

"The British Academy in Lisbon. I start on Monday. I went by the building today. It's not very large, but it looks nice."

"And the bookstore? Did you go by yet?"

"Not yet, but I'm planning to next week."

The bookstore belonged to the Hargreaves, Roger and Mary, who'd moved to Portugal some fifteen years ago and had opened a dedicated place for

English books, periodicals, and magazines. Roger and Dad had attended university together and, upon learning Simon was living in Lisbon for a while, had insisted he come by.

"It's called The Queen's English," Dad said.

"Yes, I remember."

"Anything else you've been doing?"

"Just trying to settle in and getting to know the city."

"Are you still looking for that girl?" Dad asked with a slight hesitation.

Simon closed his eyes briefly and sighed. He couldn't tell him that he'd found her and then he'd lost her again. He wasn't ready to share that when he himself was still struggling with what had happened.

"Dad, I don't want to argue with you about this again."

"I'm not arguing, Simon. I'm just interested in knowing if you've had any progress." Dad cleared his throat. "If your mother were still alive, she'd be sleuthing right along with you."

Simon chuckled. "She would, wouldn't she?" Mom had been a romantic, and this was the kind of story she would have liked. The thought comforted him.

After another pause, Simon replied. "I just have to do this, Dad. Even if nothing comes of it."

One school term. Simon gave himself three and a half months to find her again.

What were the chances in a city of almost two million people?

Chapter Four

Isabel put the tablet down on her desk and sat back. The thought pulled at her again. The letter from Elliot—she couldn't get it out of her mind.

Well, that was nothing new. After so many years writing to each other, something had shifted between them in the past twelve months. She couldn't pinpoint the moment, or even remember how it happened, but one day she'd read his letter and the feelings inside her were different. At first, the realization had caught her by surprise, but when she let herself really think about it, she was more amazed it had taken so long to admit.

His feelings were different too. The signs were there, in the carefully chosen words and the way his handwriting stressed in certain parts. Sometimes, it was between the lines, in what he left unsaid.

Or maybe it was just her imagination playing tricks on her, the heart taking over the mind and squashing reason with dreams. Of course he didn't think about her the same way she did about him. He wouldn't, would he?

She squared her shoulders and shook her head, as if the movement would knock good sense into her. She better make her way to the chairman's office than dwell on the impossible.

Was it a good sign that the academy's chairman wanted to talk to her before the regular Monday morning staff meeting? Classes had started last week, and things seemed to be faring well despite all the last-minute problems that were bound to happen at the beginning of every school year.

The door was slightly ajar when she knocked.

"Enter."

She walked through.

"Please close the door behind you, Isabel," Dr. Varela said from behind his desk. He motioned to one of the chairs, and she sat down.

He shuffled the papers on the desk for a moment, not meeting her eyes.

Isabel had been working at the academy for almost eight years now. Dr. Varela was the director who'd hired her, and she'd come to appreciate his calm demeanor and effective leadership. Managing an English-only private school required a specific set of skills that most people couldn't begin to comprehend, as she had discovered since taking the position. He'd recommended her for it, and had expressed his satisfaction numerous times, but several members of the parents' council didn't share the same opinion. Some had even tried to have her replaced.

He raised his head and stopped. "What happened to you?"

The bandages and bruises. She'd forgotten about those. "I was involved in a minor accident on Friday."

He cleared his throat. "Isabel, I brought you here before the staff meeting to give you a heads up about a new hire."

Isabel frowned. "A new teacher? Is someone leaving?" Maybe she had missed something last week.

He paused and folded his hands. "Not exactly." He cleared his throat again. "We have hired an independent consultant to overhaul the digital system at the academy."

Isabel blinked. "Overhaul the digital system? We had that done four years ago when the new online portal was introduced."

Dr. Varela hesitated. "Well, yes, that's right. But many parents have expressed their displeasure with it."

She suppressed an eye roll. "The parents' council, you mean."

He waved a hand. "Among others. But yes, the parents' council, as well as some members of the academy board. After some meetings, it was decided to hire an independent consultant to—" He paused, as if searching for the right words. "Analyze the current system, identify the weaknesses, and introduce the new system over a period of time."

Isabel watched him for a moment. It still didn't make sense. "Why was I not made aware of this?"

"Well, it was right at the beginning of summer vacation."

She nodded. When Avó Marta had passed away and Isabel had taken a week off. The first time she'd been away from the academy in her years here, and apparently they didn't need her input for important decisions. "Have there been any other concerns?"

"No, no, of course not." Dr. Varela's tone was flustered. "This will be a collaboration. You will assist him with everything he needs and he will do the same for the academy." He cast a glance at the side door. "You'll see. It'll be good for everyone."

"How long is he staying?"

"One term, to start." Again, he looked down at the desk. "It should be enough for what needs to be done, but the board will re-evaluate and take into consideration what's best for the academy. Which is all everyone wants," he added.

Isabel gave him a tight smile. "Of course."

Dr. Varela rose and walked to the side door, the one that opened to the council meeting room. "Please, come," he said to someone.

Isabel stood from her chair, and flexed her hands. Her shoulders ached, tense and taut, and she rolled them back before he returned with the other person.

A man walked in with a smile on his face. He was clearly not Portuguese, taller than most but not so tall as to draw attention. The same couldn't be said for his hair, full and red, and artfully combed as to appear he hadn't done much to it.

When she met his eyes, she gasped. "It's you."

His eyes widened in recognition. "You," he returned, watching her as if taking stock of her condition. "Are you all right? I'm so so—"

"I'm well enough, thank you," she cut in. Even though she'd been hurting and not completely in charge of her faculties, she remembered his face and his hair.

Dr. Varela cleared his throat. "I see you two have met already."

Isabel narrowed her eyes at the man in front of her. "I don't know his name."

"We haven't been introduced," the man said.

Dr. Varela took a step forward. "Isabel Antunes is the academy's director." He turned to the man. "This is Simon Ackerley, our new specialist." He looked between them again. "Did this encounter have anything to do with your accident?"

"Mr. Ackerley tried to run me over." It was beginning to make sense now. As if stealing her job wasn't enough, he was trying to get her out of the picture altogether. With her out of the way, it would be easier to take over. Only it hadn't quite worked out as he'd planned, and she didn't intend to go without a fight.

"It was an accident," he replied. "And I really am sorry for what happened on Friday."

For a long, awkward moment, the three of them stood in silence. Simon Ackerley eyed her, his expression full of something she couldn't begin to guess, almost as if he'd heard her ridiculous thoughts. It had been an accident. She didn't know where the paranoia came from.

He held out his hand to her. "Please, call me Simon."

Dr. Varela cleared his throat. "While in the building, and especially in front of the students, we address our faculty and staff as mister and miss."

Isabel shook his hand but quickly pulled her fingers away from his long ones. "Mr. Ackerley."

He smiled. "Miss Antunes. So pleased to meet you."

His accent dragged the last syllable of her name into an exaggerated sibilant. "You are not British," she said.

He shook his head, and his eyes almost twinkled. "No, I'm not."

Dr. Varela interrupted. "Mr. Ackerley is American but he's been living in England for a long time." He looked between Isabel and the man. "Well, let's not keep the others waiting. You'll have time to talk afterwards." He turned to Isabel. "I'm trusting you to give Mr. Ackerley a tour of the academy."

Isabel nodded. Of course Dr. Varela was asking her to do it. She was the one who kept abreast of everything going on at the small campus. Not as much as she thought, apparently, since the hire of this man had been a complete surprise.

When they entered the assembly room, all the teachers and other staff stopped talking and turned to them. Dr. Varela strode to the podium and gestured for Mr. Ackerley to sit in the chair behind him. Isabel followed to her usual place at the right of the podium. Cristina sat in the front row. Her mouth dropped when they entered. She lowered her hand to her side and pointed to the new guy. Isabel shook her head and mouthed *later*. Cristina nodded.

Dr. Varela covered the usual topics then finally introduced Mr. Ackerley. "And I am very pleased to introduce to you Mr. Simon Ackerley, our new specialist and Miss Antunes' assistant." He motioned with his hand. "Would you like to say a few words, Mr. Ackerley?"

Ackerley stood and approached Dr. Varela.

The blood rushed from Isabel, and her heart dropped. Mr. Simon Ackerley was her new assistant. Funny how Dr. Varela had failed to mention that. She should go back and ask Dr. Varela to explain Mr. Ackerley's position again, but that wouldn't solve anything. She clapped politely and smiled, following the lead of those in the room.

"Mr. Ackerley will be assisting Miss Antunes and assessing the demands of our school," Dr. Varela continued, as he patted Ackerley on the back.

Ackerley approached the microphone and adjusted it to his height. "Thank you, Dr. Varela, and thank you everyone for the warm welcome. I'm looking forward to working with you, and with Miss Antunes," he turned back to look at her, "and, of course, the students." He smiled again.

After a few more words from Dr. Varela, he and Ackerley descended and shook hands with some of the teachers. Isabel took the side stage, eager to leave before she was roped into any of it.

"Isabel." Cristina grabbed her arm. "It's him, isn't it?" She turned to the assembly room.

Isabel stopped and turned as well. "If you mean my new assistant, yes, it's him," she ground the words out.

Cristina stepped closer to the edge of the stage, bringing Isabel by the hand. "No, I mean the guy on the bike." She paused, watching him. "I'm pretty sure he's the biker you crashed into on Friday."

Isabel let out a slow breath. "Yes, he's the biker from Friday. He crashed into me, not the other way, remember?"

Cristina stared at him unabashedly. "Well, he sure cleans up well, doesn't he?"

Isabel looked at the guy one more time. He wore pressed green pants and a light cream button-down shirt with a ridiculous checkered necktie that some-how complimented both colors. Not many men could pull off such a style, and yet he wore it easily and with confidence. She didn't remember well, but he'd probably been wearing sports clothes on Friday.

Cristina tugged at her arm. "Let's go say hello."

Isabel pulled away. "Let's not." She walked towards the corridor. "I need to check my schedule for the week." She'd have to make changes now.

When Isabel reached her office, she closed the door and leaned against it. She inhaled deeply. Her hands were clammy and she ran them down her slacks. She stood for a few minutes, grappling with her thoughts over the recent blow.

For that's what it was. A blow to her career, to her life. After dedicating all her time to the academy for the past eight years, they had brought in someone to replace her under the guise of updating the digital system. An older, more experienced man who was a native English speaker, which was what all the parents preferred. So he wasn't British, but they would easily overlook that. Maybe he'd come to update the online portal but he wasn't here to assist her. He was here to be trained by her and then take her place. The parents' council was moving forward with their plans to remove her. She closed her eyes at the thought.

A knock sounded at the door and she jumped back. Isabel quickly walked behind her desk. "Come in."

Simon Ackerley walked in. "Miss Antunes, might we have a word, please?"

The way he said her name grated on her. "It's Antunes, not Antoo-nesh." She picked up the tablet on her desk.

"Yes, Antunes," he repeated in the same way as before. "I mean, Miss Antunes." He stood for a moment, looking at her. "Your friend was just telling me about your hospital stay and your injuries. Miss Fonseca, I think?"

Cristina and her big mouth. "That's right, Miss Fonseca. She teaches mathematics to the upper grades." Isabel paused to look at him. "And to be clear, I wasn't at the hospital for that long."

He smiled again. "I'm just glad to see you recovered. I tried to follow you to the hospital, but no one would tell me anything, and I had to stay behind to give a statement to the police officer. I wanted to make sure you were all right, and I'd like to offer to pay for any expenses incurred."

The nerve of the man. As if she couldn't pay her own bills. "Free medicine, Mr. Ackerley, just like in England," she replied smoothly. "No bill." Even if there was a bill, he wouldn't be paying for it. "But I appreciate the offer. As you said yourself, I am recovering well." Except for the soreness on her backside and the bruises under her sleeves, but she wasn't about to tell him that. She should probably take off the bandage on her hand. The younger children had a tendency to be overly interested in what lay beneath it.

She swiped at the tablet and set it down. "What can I do for you, Mr. Ackerley?"

"I'm looking forward to working with you as I introduce the needed changes to the system. Dr. Varela said no one else is more qualified than you to bring me up to date about the academy's needs."

"Of course, Mr. Ackerley. As the academy's director, I know everything that is going on." Almost everything. "I do my job well." She smoothed the sides of her blouse. "But I'm sure there's always room for improvement."

He cleared his throat. "Well said. And I'm looking forward to working with you in bringing about the best for the academy." He stuffed his hands in his pockets. "It'll be a mutually beneficial relationship."

That was too much. "Now, just hold on." Isabel came around the desk to stand in front of him. "Let's get one thing straight. We don't have a relationship of any kind. We're just co-workers. I'm being forced to train you for a job I've been working at for over three years."

"I'm not here for that," he said.

Her eyebrows rose. "Maybe you are, and maybe you're not. But if it comes to a choice between you and me, I know they'll give it to you because you're a native English-speaker and you're a man. It's not fair and I don't like it, but I can't do anything about it except do my job so well that they'll be thinking twice about bringing you in at all."

Simon held her gaze. He opened his mouth as if to say something more then closed it.

Isabel kept her posture straight. He didn't step away from her and they stood almost toe to toe. She'd worn flat, sensible shoes today when she could have used the advantage of a pair of heels. The irony. Maybe she should tuck a pair in her office for situations like this, especially if she had to work with him every day for the next three months.

He nodded at her. "Very well. As you wish. But I didn't come here to be your enemy, Miss Antunes."

She'd be the judge of that.

∽⟊⟊

Simon entered the office they'd give him and sat down. His heartbeat had slowed, but his mind was still trying to catch up to the events of the last half hour.

That moment when he'd met Isabel Antunes. He'd never forget it.

It was her, the young woman he'd been thinking about since Friday, the one who had the letter he'd sent to Amélie.

After spending all weekend berating himself for not finding out who she was, he'd hardly believed his good fortune when he saw her standing in the chairman's office.

The impression had blasted through him, louder and clearer than at any other time in his life.

It's her.

If seeing his letter with her had not been enough, now he had another confirmation. A very clear one.

He could drop the plans to put a trace on Amélie's emails, something he'd been reluctant to do in the first place. Putting together the puzzle of little clues he'd gathered over the years hadn't been as fruitful as expected. But now he didn't need any of that.

How could it possibly be? How could Isabel Antunes be his friend Amélie?

Simon shook his head. Indeed it was her.

It was an unlikely chance, but something akin to a miracle had brought him to Amélie on his first day of work. Still, he couldn't reveal himself to her. *Hi, I'm Elliot, your pen pal.* He blew out a breath, then began pacing the small space in front of the desk.

No, he couldn't. He had to prepare her first, see how she felt about meeting in person, or even find out if she was interested in meeting. There was too much to consider. He wouldn't ruin the most important friendship of his life with hastiness.

Besides, he was at the academy with the specific goal to discover who'd been siphoning small amounts of money from the academy's funds, and Dr. Varela had insisted on a confidentiality clause. The changes and improvements to the online portal were secondary and could probably be done in less than a month, but he was staying for the whole term or until the culprit was found. And now everything had just become more complicated.

He rubbed the back of his neck, as if the gesture could brush away the thoughts coursing through him. The shock hadn't quite abated yet, and probably wouldn't for some time, time he needed to think and make sense of everything.

For the time being, he had to pretend his life had not just been turned upside down.

Simon pulled out his cell phone and checked the time. The first bell would ring in ten minutes. Before he changed his mind, he walked back to Dr. Varela's office.

He knocked, barely waiting for a reply before swinging the door open. "Dr. Varela, we need to talk."

The chairman looked up from his desk and frowned. "What's the matter, Mr. Ackerley?"

Simon closed the door. "I must insist on telling Miss Antunes the true nature of my presence at the academy."

Dr. Varela waved a hand. "We already discussed this. The board feels it's better not to tell any of the faculty and staff, and I happen to agree."

"But Miss Antunes is the director and responsible for everything going on at the academy, is she not?" By not telling her he'd been hired to track the embezzler, Simon risked alienating her when she finally found out. He hadn't liked the idea before, but now with the discovery of her being Amélie, he didn't want to keep yet another secret.

"She's mostly responsible for the day-to-day management of the academy and all that it entails. She is also the liaison with the parents." Dr. Varela rested his elbows on the desk. "As the chairman, I'm the one responsible for the faculty and staff, and until you discover some clues as to the identity of the culprit, everyone is under suspicion. And that includes Miss Antunes."

"But I think—"

"Mr. Ackerley, this matter is not really up for discussion."

Simon's shoulders dropped. "Yes, sir."

"If you don't mind then, I'd rather not have to talk about this again." Dr. Varela gestured towards the door. "Isn't Miss Antunes waiting for you?"

Simon nodded and returned to his office. He stood in the small place and took a deep breath, trying to turn his mood around.

After the announcements for the week and day were read over the school's speaker, Isabel Antunes would be accompanying him on a tour of the academy and grounds. It had been his idea, to gain a sense of the place and the people, something completely different, since he usually worked behind a desk and never went on field jobs. He reached for the pad and pencil on the desk then inhaled again, rolling his shoulders to drop the tension squeezing at him. The feeling of certainty about Isabel being Amélie persisted, but he had to put it aside for now and examine it more at home.

He had not planned for things to go this way, had he? Of all the times he'd daydreamed about meeting Amélie, working with her was the furthest one from his mind. Such a turn of events.

He caught up with Isabel in the foyer of the school.

She held a large tablet against her chest and he half expected her to produce a skeleton key that opened all the doors to the realm. The mental image brought a small smile to his mouth and she quirked an eyebrow at him.

"Are you ready, Mr. Ackerley?"

"Looking forward to it, Miss Antunes."

They started the tour in the main office and reception area. "This is Miss Soares, our full-time secretary, and Miss Silva, her assistant." Simon nodded at both women. "They speak English but you'll soon find out that not all of our staff does. In most cases, we don't require bilingual employees when they have less direct contact with the students."

They left the office and took the lower hallway.

"That makes sense. How many students do you have enrolled?" He had a report somewhere in his messenger bag, but he'd rather get the facts from her.

"One hundred and sixty-three students this semester." She frowned a little. "Yes, we're a small school. We like to keep the classes small for more personal interaction between teachers and students. Classes in first through third grade have twelve to thirteen students and fourth through sixth grade average fifteen to sixteen students. The lower grade teachers have full-time assistants and the upper grades have teacher specialists that allow for rotations and class work in smaller groups."

She took him next to meet the librarian and media specialist, the head custodian, and the janitors. The kitchen had two cooks and the cafeteria two servers. Once outside on the grounds, he met the gardener who came on Mondays and Thursdays.

They stopped at the far corner of the playground where the lower grade classes enjoyed morning recess.

Simon leaned against the wall and took some notes. "How is the security handled?"

"Through an independent security company. They handle it remotely and also on site." She held up her badge. "All personnel have their own security badge and it identifies their entries and exits at the academy." She turned the badge around and showed him a key. "Dr. Varela and I have keys, as do some of the senior staff and faculty."

Dr. Varela had issued Simon a card as well, along with passwords for everything else. He slipped the notepad in his pocket and looked around the adjacent courtyard. Mature trees offered shade over several areas and scattered benches throughout presented spaces where students and teachers could sit and read. By the back door to the kitchen, raised beds with vegetables and herbs brimmed with late offerings.

Isabel followed his gaze. "Each class gets a small area to grow seeds in the early spring. The gardener waters through the summer and picks up the early harvest. The students resume their work again in September in time for the second harvest."

He nodded. "A great project for the children."

Her shoulders relaxed as she surveyed the grounds. She stood in profile to him and Simon sent her a glance disguising it as interest for the surroundings. He didn't want to be caught openly staring at her. The words they'd exchanged earlier in her office were still fresh on his mind. Under the calm appearance, her anger had been palpable, and he couldn't blame her for it. Her boss had not told her of Simon's coming before today, nor his purpose, that much was clear, and he regretted their rocky start. As eager as he was to get to know her better, patience and tact were virtues worth remembering.

After one more look around, Isabel took the path to the school and he followed.

"How long have you worked here?" Simon caught up to her. For a short woman, she walked fast. Well, shorter than most women in England. Here in Portugal she had two or three centimeters on the general female population, which would make her at the perfect height to fit nicely is his arms. The unexpected thought surprised him, and he stepped back to put more distance between them.

"It was my second job after graduating. I first worked in the administration of a public preparatory school for a few years, but when a position opened here I applied right away." She stopped at the front gate and introduced him to one of the security officers who didn't speak English. She facilitated the translation.

They ended the tour in front of their offices, tucked away at the end of a hallway around the corner from the reception foyer.

"I was first hired as an administrator here, as well, but Dr. Varela appointed me director three years ago."

"And from what I've seen today, you're doing a tremendous job of it." The compliment was genuine. His first impressions were favorable, and everything seemed to run efficiently.

Immediately, Isabel straightened and squared her shoulders. "Don't patronize me, Mr. Ackerley. Someone is obviously not pleased with my work here, or they wouldn't have called you to consult." She ground out the last word with added emphasis.

Not this again. She was determined to make him an enemy. How frustrating. "I don't think you understand what I do, Isabel." He stepped forward.

"Miss Antunes, please." She crossed her arms. "We're inside the building and need to observe the rules."

"Miss Antunes, as I said earlier, I'm not your enemy, and I don't want your position at the academy. I'm here to improve the online system. That's what I do as an IT consultant." He kept his eyes on hers. "My reports are aimed at helping the academy as a whole. Everyone will benefit, including you. My job here is to make your job easier."

"I hope so," she said. But her eyes betrayed her. She wasn't convinced.

Changing Isabel Antunes' mind about him and his presence at the academy had just moved to the top of his priority list.

Now he just needed to gain her trust and prepare her for Elliot.

CHAPTER FIVE

To: ameliefaithfulfriend@mail.com
From: elliotbestpenpal@mail.com

Dear Amélie,

I'm a little busy, but I'll always find time for you. For the time being, I'm only trying to get used to all the changes. I started on the new job and even though I'm excited about it, I'm also slightly apprehensive. There, I said it. I've been putting up a façade with everyone else, but not with you. Change is hard, even when you seek it yourself. But in this case, it's a risk worth taking.

I think you're wrong about not making a difference in the lives of those around you. I don't know the kind of job you do, but I know you always do your best. I remember how studious and applied you were in secondary school and university, always turning in homework on time and going beyond for extra *credit. It speaks of your character and I have reason to believe you give your best at everything you do.*

Hang in there. The right path will come to you, either doing the same or something new. You never know what the future holds.

Always,
Elliot

༺ঞ৹

To: elliotbestpenpal@mail.com
From: ameliefaithfulfriend@mail.com

Dear Elliot,

I'm glad to know you're excited about the new job. I'm positive you'll do great and charm everyone. What does your family say about it?

I appreciate your vote of confidence and your kind words. I wish I could feel the same way. You know the saying, "Be careful what you wish for?" Well, that's me. I wanted change and I got it. Only, it's not the kind of change I expected.

You see, I met someone. I know what you're thinking and it's not like that. SO not like that. This person is exasperating and unfortunately I can't do anything about it. I wish I could work with someone like you instead, because I'm sure you're a fun co-worker. But enough whining.

Do you miss London? When are you going back?

Your friend,
Amélie

CHAPTER SIX

Simon stretched his arms above his head and yawned. He stacked the papers and slipped them back into the folder. The academy had closed its doors two hours earlier and he was still here, going over the information he'd collected at the end of the first week. So much for a Friday night catching up with his reading list. At least he'd made some progress on entering all of the staff and faculty card numbers and digital signatures into the tracking program. As a result, he'd discovered the card used in connection with the fraudulent bank transfers. Unfortunately, he'd also found out that card belonged to Isabel.

Her involvement was not even in question. She was innocent; of that he had no doubt. But his personal conviction about her moral character was not enough to prove someone else was using the card. And until he had solid evidence, he'd hold his discovery from Dr. Varela.

Simon twirled a pencil between his fingers. Logic and common sense told him that Isabel must have left her card and key unattended at some point, creating an opportunity for someone to make a copy of it. She hadn't even noticed. It was unfortunate the academy didn't have security cameras installed in the hallway by the offices. He'd have to think of another way to find out how her card had been taken.

But not today.

He turned off the lights and locked his door. His small office sat directly in front of Isabel's. She was his biggest challenge. If he'd ever met efficiency personified, it would be her. As the director, she kept a tight rein on her little kingdom and he'd been impressed with her ability to remember the names of all the students they'd met, the mark of an involved teacher.

It wasn't his responsibility, but as the last one in the building, he took it upon himself to make sure all the lights were off and windows locked. This new habit had him walking through the back part of the school before he left for the day. When he turned to the second hallway, light shone through the porthole on the service door to the kitchen. Simon stopped. Had one of the cooks stayed behind?

He approached the door and peeked through. Someone stood near the stove, with her back to him. She had her brown hair piled up and wore a black T-shirt and a yellow apron tied twice around her waist. Her exposed neck gave him a clear view of a small tattoo at the nape. Something he couldn't make out from this far. Simon pushed open the door and cleared his throat. "Excuse me, are you one of the cooks?" Hopefully, she spoke English.

She didn't turn, but she moved side to side and hummed something. Thin red cords for earbuds dangled from her ears.

Simon clapped his hands and raised his voice. "Excuse me!"

The woman jumped and screamed. She turned around, a large chef knife in her right hand.

Simon raised his hands and stepped back. "Easy there. It's just me."

Isabel yanked at the cords and the earbuds dropped to the floor. "Are you out of your blessed mind?" She spoke slowly in a low tone, almost a growl. Her eyes narrowed. "Did you not see my chopping knife?" She set it down on the wood block, then bent and picked up the earbuds which she stuffed into the apron pocket. "What are you doing here? Other than scaring me to death and trying to get yourself killed."

Simon took a quick breath. "I'm sorry, but I didn't see the knife. In fact, I didn't even recognize you." She looked younger in simple jeans, form-fitting jeans, the kind that hugged her figure in all the right places. The black t-shirt looked just as good. It read *I cook: what's your super power?* in white letters across the chest. Simon suppressed a smile. Even her hair looked different, softer and more relaxed. She always wore it in a tight, low bun during school hours. But here, in front of him, Isabel had an alter-ego, a very appealing one.

She brought her hands to her hips. "You didn't answer me."

"I was doing the rounds before I left. I certainly didn't expect to find anyone in the kitchen, least of all you." Simon leaned against the stainless steel counter. "What are you doing here?"

She rubbed her temples and sighed, then caught herself and straightened. "You're going to tell on me, aren't you?"

The oven timer beeped behind her, and she waved him off. "Move over there, please, and don't say anything for a minute."

Simon walked behind the counter and pulled up a bar stool from under a corner. He sat and watched her while he waited for her to finish. Maybe he'd have the chance to talk with her, a subject beyond the academy, the system, and the students.

She took four white ceramic dishes and placed them on a baking sheet. Then she moved to the other side and brought over a large glass bowl with a dark chocolate batter, which she carefully spooned inside the round, ribbed dishes. She slid the tray into the oven and set the timer.

For a minute, she stood in front of the oven. Was she going to watch while they baked?

The tattoo at the base of her neck was a small trail of stars that disappeared down her back and underneath the T-shirt. This woman was a contradiction, so stiff and proper, yet mysterious and captivating. Simon pushed the thought away. He couldn't think of her like this, not at work.

After placing the bowl and utensils in the sink and running some water over them, she turned to face him.

"Are you a chef?" Simon asked.

She shook her head and actually rolled her eyes. "Are you going to tell on me?" She repeated the question.

"What's there to tell? You're in the kitchen, baking something."

She nodded.

"Is there something wrong about it?"

She shook her head. "Technically, I'm not supposed to."

That would account for her guilty demeanor.

Her shoulders dropped. "Look, Mr. Ackerley—"

"Simon," he said. "It's after hours. Call me Simon."

She crossed her arms again. "As I was saying, Mr. Ackerley." The two last words came out accented, then she paused, took a breath, and started again. "My late grandmother was friends with the main cook. They were best friends, actually. My oven at home broke, and while the technician is waiting for the part, my grandmother's friend agreed to let me use the kitchen here. As long as I'm not cooking for any official business and clean everything after me, she doesn't mind."

Simon nodded. "So this is a one-time thing?"

She nibbled at her thumb. "Yes, it should be."

"All right." So Isabel was using the academy's kitchen, and she didn't look too happy that he'd found her.

She paused and looked at him. "Look, I'd just rather people don't know that I cook. Don't you ever do anything to de-stress?"

Simon smiled. "Yeah, I go bike riding."

"Do you make a habit of crashing into pedestrians as well?"

"That was the first time."

"Just my luck," she deadpanned.

No, it had been his luck but she wouldn't understand, and he kept it to himself.

"I cook and bake. Or I cooked and baked before my oven broke. You're going to tell the chairman you caught me here and I'll be lucky if I don't lose my job." She turned to the sink and washed the dirty bowl.

Simon rose and came to stand near the sink. "I'm not going to tell on you, Isabel." She looked at him pointedly, but didn't comment. "Believe it or not, I do understand about doing something to unwind." He moved out of the way when she placed the clean utensils on a drying rack and started wiping them down with paper towels. "And you are the school director, after all. If you can't use the kitchen, then I don't know who can."

"And you're the director's assistant," she said without turning.

Simon wanted to tell her that didn't mean anything, but he kept quiet instead. He didn't want to argue with her and she seemed to be in the mood to contradict.

She worked quickly, washing, drying, and putting pieces of equipment back in their places. Once or twice, she looked his way, opened her mouth as if to say something, and then closed it. Maybe she was doing something she liked, but she wasn't relaxed in his presence.

Before the timer went off, she turned off the gas stove and waited. When it beeped, she reached a gloved hand for the tray and set it on the counter. The batter had popped over the rims, dark brown and enticing.

"What are those?"

She poured confectioner's sugar into a small sieve. "Chocolate soufflés," she said in a low voice.

Slowly, she moved two of the dishes from the tray to their own white plates, then dusted their tops, the edge of her finger hitting the side of the small sieve with a few taps. She took a pinch from a small bowl and added the contents to the top of each soufflé. She stood back and smiled at them.

"Did you just smile at your dessert?"

A scowl quickly replaced her smile. She reached in her pocket and checked her phone. "Cristina was supposed to be here, but she bailed on me with her boyfriend." She put the phone back. "Which is only fair since last week she bailed on him to take care of me after some biker mowed me down."

"You have no idea how worried I was about you all weekend." He hadn't meant to confess it with so much emotion in his voice.

Isabel raised an eyebrow but didn't comment. She placed a dessert spoon on the plate and pushed it in his direction. "Looks like you're my guinea pig tonight, Mr. Ackerley."

Simon pulled the plate closer and touched the top of the batter. It was warm, and a soft aroma wafted to him. The soufflé sprang back at the first contact with the spoon and Simon pressed harder. The batter had turned airy and spongy, and when he took a bite, his eyes closed.

"Mmmm." He actually moaned. When was the last time he'd moaned about food? "Wow, you do have super powers." His eyes flicked to the front of her T-shirt.

"Hardly." She looked at him expectantly. "Well, is that all you're going to say?"

Simon scraped the bottom of the dish. "It has a sweet, full flavor. It's fluffy too."

"Did you just say fluffy, Mr. Ackerley?" She didn't hide the amusement in her tone.

He set the spoon down and resisted the urge to wipe his mouth with the back of his hand. "Yes, Isabel, I said fluffy. But I hardly have the words to describe this piece of culinary perfection."

She placed another soufflé on his plate. "Have another one. These won't keep." Then she pulled a small notebook out of her apron pocket and wrote some notes while eating her own soufflé at a leisurely pace.

Simon watched her as he ate. He had found a chink in her armor. A delicious chink. "Where did you learn to bake like this?" Once again, he scraped the bottom and licked the spoon a few times.

Without hesitation, she placed the last soufflé in front of him.

"No, I couldn't," he said weakly.

"Yes, you can."

"Thank you," he replied, picking up his spoon and sliding it slowly into the little piece of chocolate heaven. He didn't even pretend to put on any kind of resistance.

For a moment, her mask slipped and she watched him with relish, as if his pleasure in the dessert she'd created was the highest form of praise.

"I seriously can't remember eating something so good," he said, wishing he could lick the inside of the small dish. "Do you have a secondary degree in the culinary arts?"

Her shoulders pulled back. "My grandmother taught me what she knew." She turned back to the sink as she washed his dish and spoon. "I taught myself the rest. I've been trying to perfect this recipe for almost a year now, but I don't think it's there yet."

"If it's not perfect yet, I would like to be there when you achieve perfection." Her cheeks colored and before her defenses rose, he went on. "Is that what you're writing down in that notebook? Your results?"

She drew it closer to her, as if he could read what she'd written. Even if he could distinguish the words, she most likely wrote in Portuguese and he didn't know the language. "When something doesn't turn out as I expected, I write it down so I know what to work on next time."

"Do you also write your guinea pigs' responses?"

She frowned. "Excuse me?"

"You said I was your guinea pig today and I absolutely loved it."

That he'd loved this time spent with her more than the chocolate soufflé was something he'd keep to himself.

༄

Isabel pushed open the familiar oak doors, the scent of printed pages and literary friends momentarily stronger than the aroma from the café next door.

The Queen's English bookstore catered to English-speaking readers, the only one of its kind in Lisbon. From classics to the latest bestsellers, daily newspapers, magazines—anything that was printed in the English language, they carried at least one copy. Or so they boasted. They certainly had the space, with a main room at street level, and an upstairs room where the owners hosted a weekly book club before opening later on Sundays.

She waved at Mary Hargreaves as she made her way up the narrow staircase, balancing a container full of orange madeleines she'd managed to bake the night before. Mary and her husband Roger had come to Lisbon from London for a fortnight vacation and had never left, too entranced with the mild weather and the good food, as they would recount to anyone who asked. Isabel had found the quaint shop, housed in a tastefully restored early-20th century building, when she'd needed a particular copy of a hard-to-find edition of Walden Pond, and before long she'd joined the eclectic club.

This month's book selection was *Far From the Madding Crowd*, and Isabel was holding judgment until she finished her reading, although some of the other club members most likely wouldn't.

As the meeting wound to a close, Roger Hargreaves excused himself and walked downstairs. The meeting had turned into a surprisingly sedate discussion due to the absence of a couple of members who tended to be more vocal. Still, Isabel had struggled to keep her attention, her thoughts straying to the changes at work and to the new man the academy had hired.

Was there a valid reason for her concern? How could she trust the newcomer when she suspected his motives?

The others walked to the side table where the refreshments had been laid out, including the madeleines she'd brought.

"These are the best, Isabel," Nancy Parson said after taking a bite. She taught English Literature at a local university.

"Thanks, Peggy," Isabel replied from her seat, the book still open on her lap.

Mary Hargreaves nodded at Isabel with a smile, her mouth too full to talk.

The sound of footsteps and voices coming up the stairs gradually filled the room. Roger Hargreaves laughed and a man beside him did the same.

"Everyone," said Roger, "This is Simon Ackerley, the son of an old friend of mine."

Isabel grabbed her book and lifted it up to cover her face. What was he doing here? Of all the places in the city, all the things to see and do on a Sunday, did he have to come to the one thing she did?

As the others approached and the Hargreaves made introductions, Isabel remained in her chair, wishing she'd picked up a coffee table book instead of a pocket edition. It was only a matter of time before they called her over.

"What are these called, Isabel?"

She rose, clutching the book to her middle and suppressing a deep sigh. "Those are orange madeleines," she replied. "I baked them last night."

"These are delicious," said a familiar deep voice.

Roger touched her elbow and prodded her forward. "Have you met Simon? He's fresh from London. Simon, this is Isabel Antunes and she works at the English Academy."

Simon's eyes widened but he recovered quickly and shook her hand, smiling. "What a pleasant surprise, Isabel."

Why did he have such nice, long fingers? Isabel returned the shake and suddenly wished she had something to fan herself. It felt like someone had upped the heat, though autumn had barely started. His green eyes smiled at her and even his freckles looked different today. The necktie was a mustardy color and it matched ridiculously well with his suit and eyes. Did he dress with the aid of a color wheel? Most likely he had a fashion-savvy girlfriend waiting for him in England. Or maybe she'd come along too.

Mary joined her husband and they both looked on with quizzical expressions.

"We already know each other," Simon Ackerley said with a twitch to his lips.

Isabel glanced at the clock on the wall, mentally calculating how soon she could leave.

"How wonderful. Where did you meet?" Mary asked.

"At the academy," she and Ackerley replied at the same time.

Simon Ackerley spent the next few minutes answering the Hargreaves' questions about his work and her work and what they did at the academy. Isabel tuned out, nodding when they looked in her direction. How much longer did she have to stay? She just had to think of an excuse and she'd be on her way. Her eyes darted around.

A knock sounded at the front door of the store and Mary rushed down the stairs. "I forgot opening time," she said.

Isabel took the chance and excused herself, then retrieved her purse. She waved a hasty goodbye to everyone and slipped out the front door into the sunny day.

Once outside she took a breath and touched her forehead. The one place she didn't think she'd see him and here he was.

She'd come to the book club looking for a reprieve, a bit of time to do something different and take her mind off the week she'd had at work. She didn't feel her position there was as safe as she'd believed, and everyday brought a level of stress she wasn't used to. Simon Ackerley's presence at the bookstore was a reminder of everything that had gone wrong.

Lisbon was such a large city and they kept bumping into each other. Was she overreacting in feeling frustrated? He'd called her Isabel, of course, since they'd not been at the academy.

As unfair as it was to blame him for upsetting her plans today, she didn't have the courage to stay and expose her vulnerable heart to more emotional strain. It was better she left. At least he could enjoy the time with Roger and Mary Hargreaves.

"How long have you been coming to the book club?" Ackerley said at her side.

Isabel jumped. "Stop sneaking up on me."

He held his hands up, a contrite expression on his face. "Sorry. I thought you knew I was right behind you."

"You just got there so I thought you stayed." Isabel started walking down the street.

"I'm going back later," he said, easily keeping pace with her. "They invited me for dinner.

"You're welcome to go back now," Isabel said, hoping he took her suggestion.

She glanced at him and his lips quirked. "I'll walk with you a little bit, if you don't mind."

She did mind, but saying so would be rude. As long as he didn't intend to follow her home, she wouldn't say anything. A public garden lay ahead and maybe she could lose him there.

Isabel headed for a bench in the shade of a bougainvillea, and she sat down, purse in her lap. Ackerley paused for a moment and then sat at the other end.

"Are you mad at me because I called you Isabel back at the bookstore?" he asked after a long moment. Before she could think of what to say, he went on. "Well, we're not at the academy, so I won't call you Miss Antunes."

"You still don't know how to say Antunes right." It was petulant and childish, and she couldn't stop herself. Her heart twisted with a pinch of guilt over the way she'd treated him at the academy. She'd watched him around all week. He was always cheerful and ready with a smile. He really was one of the good guys. It would be so much easier to dislike him if he were a rude, older man. Why did he have to be good looking, polite, and so pleasant to be around? Already the students loved him and went out of their way to greet him every day.

He leaned back and crossed his ankle over his knee. "What about Isabel? Do I say that right?"

Too well for her liking. And his accent— much too charming for his own good. Funny, since she usually preferred a British accent.

Isabel nodded at him. "To answer your question, Mr. Ackerley, I've been attending the book club for about three years now."

"Call me Simon, please. We're not at the academy."

He was persistent, she gave him that. "Simon."

His eyes lit up and his expression brightened, as if her saying his name was the best thing that had happened to him all day. Isabel couldn't even remember the last time someone had smiled at her with such happiness. Why did it matter so much to him?

Isabel's phone rang. She pulled it out of her purse to see who it was and then clicked it shut.

Simon quirked an eyebrow. "Don't you have to take that?"

"It's my cousin Jacinta. I'll call her later."

"Would that be Jacinta Antunes?"

His effort on the pronunciation didn't quite achieve the desired result, but it was getting marginally better.

"No, our mothers were sisters. It's mostly us on the Silva side of the family, but she has a lot of Romano cousins."

"Romano is a lot easier to say," Simon said.

"She's married. Her name is Jacinta Campbell now."

Simon's eyes shot up when he heard the last name. "Campbell?"

"Her husband is American."

"Maybe you could introduce me sometime." As casually as he said the words, his eyes belied an interest she didn't quite understand.

"They live in Porto, but I'll ask her if they have plans to come down for a visit."

He only nodded.

A soft breeze blew and a few pink petals from the bougainvillea fell on her skirt. Isabel inhaled the sweet aroma. It was a beautiful Sunday afternoon. If Avó Marta were still alive, they would have taken a walk to the historic downtown and stopped by the river's edge.

"I couldn't help notice you said your mothers were sisters," he said after a pause.

He hadn't missed the past tense. "My parents died in a car crash when I was three years old and my grandmother raised me. I was their only child."

"Is your grandmother the only family you have here in Lisbon?"

Isabel shook her head. "She passed away last year."

"I'm sorry," he said in a soft voice. "Do you have anyone else?"

"Not in the area." Isabel twisted the strap of her purse between her fingers. "There's someone who's almost family, but they don't live close by." She paused and took a breath. "I don't know why I'm telling you all this." It was becoming a bad habit, this tendency to open up to him. Something she rarely did with anyone else.

Simon looked down at his shoes. "My mother—" He hesitated for a moment and then looked back to Isabel. "My mother passed away when I was fifteen."

"I'm sorry," Isabel said. They didn't need to say anything else to know exactly what the other was feeling.

A young couple with a toddler walked by and Simon and Isabel's attention shifted to the distraction as the parents held on to the child's hands, the three of them laughing.

That had been Isabel's life for a few years, before the accident claimed her parents' lives. How much different would her own life had been if they'd lived? If Avó Marta hadn't died so young?

A tear teased her eye lashes and Isabel swiped at it impatiently. If only she were stronger…

Simon's voice interrupted her musings. "You're a strong woman, Isabel."

She startled and turned to him. "Why do you say that?" How did he know her thoughts and feelings?

He shrugged. "Just a hunch." Simon uncrossed his legs and leaned in her direction. "Without the support of close family and with a demanding job such as yours, I think you're stronger than you give yourself credit for."

She didn't say anything for a moment, as she swallowed the lump in her throat. "That sounds like something Grandmother would have said."

Nobody had said anything that nice to her in a long time.

CHAPTER SEVEN

To: ameliefaithfulfriend@mail.com
From: elliotbestpenpal@mail.com

Dear Amélie,
My family thinks I'm bonkers but what else is new, right?

I do miss London but I'm happy here too. I'm getting over my fear of strangers while trying not to scare the natives. It's a hard balance, but I'm making progress.

My new job is going well and my co-workers seem to enjoy my company. If they don't, they hide it from me. I'm sorry for you that you work with difficult individuals. I know it's not much fun, believe me.

Today I walked to the local park and had lunch under a tree. Autumn will be here in a few weeks, but the weather is still nice, and I wanted to enjoy it out-of-doors after a whole week inside. I actually laid on the grass and sunbathed for a little while.

I had time to think about my family and my life and where I'm going. Do you ever have a moment to stop and think, Amélie? It's sobering, in a way. It made me realize how small I am in the grand scheme of things, but at the same time I play an important role, especially as I put my hands to use in helping others around me. It reminded me of what you said a few weeks ago.

What are your plans for the weekend? I should say Sunday, since Saturday is almost gone. I miss your day trips. Tell me about the exciting places in Lisbon.

As always,

Elliot

೧൴

To: elliotbestpenpal@mail.com
From: ameliefaithfulfriend@mail.com

Dear Elliot,
My moments to think come in the early morning just before the alarm goes off. I'm barely awake and still clinging to my dreams, and my mind fights running a schedule for the day. I push it off and burrow under the sheets

a little longer. That's when I think. Maybe even I can call it meditation.

We must live parallel lives for I too had a week mostly indoors and went out a little bit on the weekend. The weather has been nice here as well. Autumn is pushing its way in and summer is resisting for a while longer, which is fine by me.

There's so much to do and see in Lisbon! I've lived my whole life here and I never get tired of it. It can be too much in the full summer season with so many tourists around. I really like it when they start going home, which is a bit selfish to say.

I like to walk in the shopping district and look at the windows. There's a small store called O Hospital das Bonecas, The Doll Hospital. They fix and clean dolls and stuffed animals of all kinds, and they make them look like new again. I loved going by when I was little. Sometimes I wonder if I'll ever have the chance to take a child of mine there.

Well, I'm getting too sentimental.

Your old friend,

Amélie

Chapter Eight

Simon grabbed a tray from the cafeteria and walked to his office to eat lunch. Monday was only half way done and already they'd dealt with more problems than the previous weeks. Three cars clashed in a fender bender during morning drop-offs; a class pet vanished in fifth grade, and two of the first graders had puked at lunch. He'd smoothed things over with the traffic police, he'd retrieved the guinea pig from behind a cupboard, and the janitors had taken care of the problem in the cafeteria. He was glad he'd missed that one.

He sat at his desk and silenced his phone. Isabel was off campus trying to hire a plumbing company to come fix a bathroom issue in the upper grade hall, and he'd happily stayed behind to manage the academy in her absence. Just their luck that the full-time maintenance guy was out sick, as he'd found out in the past hour. Simon had turned off the water to the girls' bathroom in the upper hall and rerouted the girls to use the facilities in the lower grades' hall. They didn't like it much but it was better than no bathrooms at all, as he had reminded them.

Meanwhile, the chairman had a family emergency and nobody knew when he'd return. Simon wasn't too worried about it. Isabel managed the day-to-day at the academy, and she did it very well. He was there to help with anything she needed. That's why they'd hired him, after all, even if his job description didn't include crawling after pets.

His cell phone rattled on the desk. Simon put down his bowl of rice and tapped the screen. It was a text from the secretary: **There's a situation in the boys' bathroom, Mr. Ackerley**.

Simon walked out of his office and around the corner to where she sat. "What situation?"

She shrugged. "I'm not sure. One of the boys came over to tell me but I can't leave my desk."

Simon pocketed his phone. "It's okay. I'll check into it. Did Miss Antunes come back yet?"

She looked up from the computer screen. "Not yet, but she did send a message saying the plumber should be here soon."

Good news. Hopefully they could get the issue fixed quickly.

When Simon approached the bathrooms, the sound of water running reached his ears before he entered. The girls' bathrooms were still roped off. He pushed the door to the boys' bathrooms. The faucets in the sinks were turned off and so were the urinals. But the toilets in the stalls had running water coming from the flush tanks and well on its way toward the door. As Simon moved to turn off all the valves, the water overflowed and spilled onto his shoes, his best pair of light brown leather wingtips.

An incoming text vibrated his phone: **The plumber has arrived, Mr. Ackerley.**

Let him in, please, he replied.

Simon shook his feet in vain. He was soaked to his ankles. Out in the hallway, he bent down and rolled up the hem of his pants just as the plumber turned the corner. He looked at Simon and said something in Portuguese. Simon gestured to the girls' bathroom first then turned the other way to the fifth and sixth grade classes.

He knocked at the door of the sixth grade classroom and addressed the teacher. "I'm sorry for the interruption." He turned to the students. "Does anyone know what happened in the bathrooms?"

Several students looked away from him, while others sent furtive glances around. The blushing cheeks and guilty looks were enough to tip him off that some of them did know what caused the toilets to overflow. "Okay, class captains, come with me." Maybe if he brought them to the bathrooms, he could get a confession.

The teacher gestured at the door. "Please follow Mr. Ackerley."

The oldest boy and girl stood from their desks and walked out with him. Simon stopped at the fifth grade class and repeated the directive. The four students followed behind him, trading glances and shrugs and murmuring in Portuguese, even though they all knew it was against the rules.

As they turned in the direction of the bathrooms, Isabel was already by the door.

She gestured at the boys' bathrooms. "What's going on here?"

Simon's shoulders relaxed. "That's what I'm trying to find out." He held the door open for her. "The plumber is already in there. I'll stay with these students."

A few moments later, Isabel pushed the door and the plumber followed behind holding a bucket in his hand. Isabel talked animatedly in Portuguese and the guy nodded. The students stepped back and turned bright red. They definitely knew more than they'd admitted.

Isabel called for Simon. The plumber had pulled out the cover for the toilet tank and was in the process of extracting something from the interior.

"What is that?" Simon asked.

The plumber set it on the floor. It was made of a semi-rigid see-through plastic and there were streaks of color on it, now running on both sides.

Isabel tapped it with the tip of her shoe. "That, Mr. Ackerley, looks to be some kind of ghost character that hangs around in the bathrooms."

Simon looked at the floor where the strange object lay in a heap. The round glasses, the long hair in low pony tails. Just like the movie character.

Isabel walked past him. When Simon reached the hallway, she had the students lined up against the wall.

"Well, Mr. Ackerley is here now, so who's going to tell him what happened?" Her face was flushed but she didn't raise her voice. At the continued silence, she touched the watch on her wrist. "We're wasting everybody's time, ladies and gentlemen. I advise you to confess right now. Class captains?"

The oldest boy and girl raised their heads. The boy spoke first. "The boys put trolls in the toilet bowls of the girls' bathrooms."

The girl looked between him and Isabel. "And the girls put the moaning myrtles in the flush tanks of the boys' bathroom."

Simon looked at them for a moment. "How did you even make these?"

"We used the 3D printer in the science lab," said the sixth grade girl.

Isabel crossed her arms. "And where did you get the design?"

The fifth grade boy spoke up. "That was me. I came up with the design."

Isabel exhaled loudly and pinched the bridge of her nose. After a moment, she turned to the students. "For the time being, I'm issuing demerits for all the students in both classes. We'll talk about this later when Mr. Ackerley and I have discussed a proper consequence for this inexcusable behavior. Now, go back to class."

After some instructions to the plumber, she left the bathrooms and Simon followed her down the hallway.

"That's some serious talent these kids have," he said. "Now we just need to redirect their focus to something productive."

"Don't worry. I intend to talk to the science and computer specialists about this." She stopped and looked down at his feet. "What happened to you? You're sloshing."

"An unfortunate consequence of the bathroom pranks."

"Pity. Those were nice shoes." She opened the door to her office.

They weren't nice shoes anymore.

After the last bell rang, Simon waited by the front door of the academy. His pants had half-dried and the secretary had brought him a pair of flip-flops. He suspected Isabel was behind the gesture, but couldn't get it confirmed.

She stood outside, saying goodbye to the students and waving at the parents, probably making sure the parents and guardians kept their heads and didn't get into more fender benders. As if anyone would dare do anything against the rules in her presence. How she managed to instill respect and affection at the same time baffled him.

She returned a few minutes later. "You're free to

leave, Mr. Ackerley."

"I'll do the rounds with you." It was something they could each do by themselves, but he preferred to do it in her company.

She flicked a glance at his feet. "As long as you can keep up in those." Was that a little smile?

"Not a problem. And thanks for sending them, by the way." Simon trailed behind her as she turned off overhead lights and locked classroom doors.

"Why do you think it was me who sent them?"

"I asked the secretary how you knew my shoe size and she said she had no idea." So maybe it had been a bit of a trick question.

She tsked. "It's so hard to find good help these days."

Simon cocked his head. Was she serious?

Isabel chuckled lightly. "Relax, Mr. Ackerley, I'm only teasing. Miss Soares is the best secretary I could ask for. She's very well compensated for her hard work, I can tell you that."

"Either way, my feet thank you for the flip-flops."

She waited for him to retrieve his messenger bag and a plastic sack containing his water-logged socks and ruined shoes.

When they locked the front gate, she turned to him. "I didn't do it for you alone, you know. I was getting tired of the sloshing sound in the hallway."

At the little hint of a smile, Simon chuckled.

They stopped at the top of the street and she turned to him. "I wanted to thank you for holding down the fort while I was away this morning."

Her expression was open and friendly and its effect on Simon had him wishing he could step forward and hug her. He slipped his free hand in his pocket instead. "No need to thank me, just doing my job." It had been a busy morning, for sure.

"Well, you had everything running smoothly by the time I came back. I wouldn't have known anything out of the ordinary ever happened."

"Except for the bathrooms situation," he reminded her.

"The sixth graders owe you a pair of shoes, Mr. Ackerley." She strode to the crosswalk.

"We're not at the academy, Isabel. Call me Simon," he said after her.

She gave him a thumbs up before crossing.

～∞～

Isabel sat on the stage facing Simon Ackerley during the morning meeting in the assembly room while the sixth graders led the announcements. He wore caramel corduroy pants, an olive green button-down shirt, and an eggplant necktie. The fifth and sixth graders had worked off their debt and bought him a new pair of brown leather wingtips, which he also wore.

Once again, he'd pulled off the style effortlessly. Even his hair color was not an issue. From this distance, the shirt enhanced his eyes. He turned her way and smiled. She wasn't staring; she was only looking at the students to make sure nobody was absent today. He could very well wipe the smirk off his face.

He was too efficient in his abilities. Some days, Isabel couldn't make up her mind whether she appreciated it or disliked it. On any other person, it would be a quality worth admiring. But the better Simon did his job, the more redundant Isabel felt. How long would it take before they asked her to resign?

Isabel bit her lip. And just how paranoid was she? His work ethic was irreproachable and he hadn't done anything for which he didn't have a reason and an explanation. It was the board's fault for placing them in a situation where she felt the need to prove her worth. She didn't like the tension it created and she liked even less how distrustful she'd become. Most days, she wanted to like Simon, and not wonder if he had any hidden motives. Like right now—why did he smile so irresistibly at her? Did he do it on purpose to rattle her?

No, of course not. That was ridiculous. He was not that kind of man. Isabel shook her head and redirected her thoughts. She needed the strength to be patient and honest and, more importantly, fair.

Cristina leaned over to her. "Eggplant with light brown polka dots," she said in a hushed tone.

Isabel looked her way. "What are you talking about?"

"Mr. Ackerley's socks. Haven't you noticed how he coordinates his socks with his neckties and the rest of his clothes?"

Yes, she'd noticed, but she wouldn't be admitting to it. "I have better things to do with my time than keep track of Mr. Ackerley's choice of socks."

Cristina smiled. "Well, the kids love it. The first graders in Miss Perry's class asked him to stop every morning to show his socks, and even my classes have started running statistical reports on the probabilities of his neckties and socks. At his suggestion, I might add." She looked in his direction again. "A genius strategy of applied math. I was jealous I didn't think of it first."

"He's been here for over a month already. The kids will run out of stats soon." Isabel turned away and faced the stage. "Besides, how many crazy socks can one man own?"

"That's what the kids are trying to find out." Cristina winked.

Did he always wear such clothes or did he dress more conservatively in other social settings? Isabel shook her head. She indeed had better things to do than spending any of her time thinking about Simon Ackerley's wardrobe.

Her phone pinged and she swiped the screen. From the secretary: **Miss Nesbitt has called in sick.**

Isabel turned to Cristina. "I need to find a substitute. The second grade teacher is sick." She walked back to her office.

Isabel called down the whole list, but didn't find anyone available. She'd have to split the class among the neighboring classes. She stood and made her way to the first and second grade hall to talk to the teachers.

When she returned, the door was ajar, and Simon stood inside by her desk. She stopped. Her hands tightened on the class list.

"Mr. Ackerley, is there something you need?"

He turned to her with a puzzled expression. "Do you always leave your door open?"

"Excuse me? What is this about?"

"The door to your office was ajar."

Isabel folded her arms and raised her chin. "And that was an invitation for you to come in and scope out the office?"

"No," he said firmly. "That's not—" He blew out a long breath and lowered his voice. "I'm just assessing the accessibility of the offices and other rooms in the academy. It's a security matter." He walked to the door.

She narrowed her eyes at him. He was hiding something. "Is that everything?"

Simon passed a hand through his hair and his expression softened for a moment. "I heard you're in need of a substitute."

Isabel put the paper down on her desk. "Unfortunately, my regular substitutes are all busy today. There's one who can come after lunch, but I'll have to split the class till then."

"If you have no objections, I'll take them," he said.

"Are you serious?"

"I'm already here and there's nothing urgent on my schedule. Why not put me to good use?"

Isabel looked at him for a long moment. As much as she wanted to press him for the reason he'd been in her office, filling in the absence for the sick teacher was more important.

Isabel walked around her desk. "Well then, Mr. Ackerley. Let's get you acquainted with those kids."

At the mid-morning recess, Isabel paused by the glass door and looked out to the playground. A smile teased her lips. Simon Ackerley was outside with the second grade class, holding one end of a jump rope for a line of waiting girls. She'd hesitated to accept his offer to substitute, but she was glad she'd changed her mind. It proved to be a good thing, a very good thing. Simon Ackerley was an excellent teacher.

"Will you look at that?" Cristina said by her side. "Could he be any more adorable?"

Isabel crossed her arms. "You mean the kids are adorable."

Cristina swatted Isabel's arm. "Why are you so determined not to like the man? I don't see anything wrong with him." She ticked her fingers. "He has a great sense of fashion, he's a dedicated worker, the kids love him. And maybe he's not British, but his manners are very gentleman-like."

Isabel had noticed that. There wasn't much she could fault him for. But she had to remember what he was doing at the academy, observing and taking notes and placing her position in peril.

"And you know what they say. You can always tell a man's personality by the way he treats his mother and how he interacts with children."

"His mother is dead," Isabel said, remembering their conversation. Fifteen was so young to lose a beloved parent.

Cristina turned to her. "He told you about his mother's death? Aren't you two getting cozy?"

Isabel ignored the comment. She watched Simon pass the rope to an older girl and jump in himself, laughing with the children. How did he manage to make jumping rope so easy and attractive? She shook her head.

Cristina gestured towards the playground. "Well, he can't get any more genuine than that. I have a feeling he'd treat his mother just right if she was around." She paused and then turned to Isabel. "Is pizza night still on?"

Isabel nodded and Cristina turned and left down the hallway.

He was waving at her. He'd caught her staring again, and he had the second graders smiling and waving at her.

Absolutely not adorable.

CHAPTER NINE

To: ameliefaithfulfriend@mail.com
From: elliotbestpenpal@mail.com

Dear Amélie,
I'm glad you've brought up the subject of meditation
and thinking. I've been wanting to talk to you about it
and not quite knowing how to do it. (Maybe we should
revisit these "rules" we set up years ago. They're kind of
ancient, anyway.)

There was a time when I was mad at life and those around
me. I blamed everyone for something that happened and
I couldn't accept it.

It took me a while to understand that people make their
own choices and there's nothing I can do about that. I can
only change my thoughts and my actions, and the way

I react to those. Whether I like the way other people act and respond or not, it's not up to me to change them.

Next time you wake up in the early morning, think positive thoughts, Amélie. Trust in yourself to know your worth.

It's all right to be sentimental once in a while. It's part of growing old, I guess. I too think about getting married and having a kid or two but my track record with relationships is not very good. Sure, I've dated and I've had girlfriends, but it's hard finding someone who shares the same values. And when you think you do find someone, she's not ready to accept everything about you. So I remain single for the time being.

Well, I'd better move on to other subjects before you tell me I'm getting too personal.

So a hospital for dolls, huh? Is that what inspired your career? I think you're giving me little clues about your job. How many shifts are you working this week, nurse Amélie? Or is it doctor Amélie? :)

Your friend always,
Elliot

∽

To: elliotbestpenpal@mail.com
From: ameliefaithfulfriend@mail.com

Dear Elliot,

Your guess is wrong. I'm not a nurse, nor a doctor, nor do I work in the medical field in any way or form. I'll give you a real clue: what I do is not exactly a nine-to-five job. ;) If you guess, I won't deny it, but I won't make it easy for you.

Are you going to give me a clue about your job as well? Or maybe a clue about where you are right now? What does the sky look like when you get up in the morning? There was a blue sky in Lisbon today, and some thin white clouds, wispy and fluffy, and almost spring-like.

I haven't gone out on a date in a long, long time. First, I'm too busy. Second, my last boyfriend told me he didn't like the person I grew into (ouch!), but I think he wanted more from me than what I was willing to give him (and not just what you're thinking about). It turned out to be a relief when he ended the relationship, and I was disappointed in myself that I stayed with him for that long. Live and learn, right?

Since then, I haven't met many guys, but I must confess I'm not trying too hard to go out and meet them. It's so much work! My friend says I'm not putting any effort into it and she's right. Maybe I'll try online dating instead. What do you think? Not all guys are as easy to talk to as you are but maybe not meeting in person takes the pressure off a bit.

I'm always talking about bravery, as long as it's others being brave. Maybe it's time I try something brave myself. I could go out and strike up a conversation with a guy. Or maybe I'll try to be nice to someone I already know. Or I could set up a profile on a dating site.

In other news, I started rereading Harry Potter. I want to know if it's as great as I found it to be when I was in school. I hope it is.

Your rambling friend,
Amélie

CHAPTER TEN

*P*izza night. Cristina had come up with the idea one time after a long day at the academy, and Isabel had offered to host it. The new part for the oven had finally come and the technician had installed it with two days to spare. Isabel had made the dough in the morning and had it rolled out in floured baking sheets. The shrimp waited in the pan for a last minute sauté and the vegetables and other toppings were arranged on the counter in square ceramic bowls.

Cristina arrived with her boyfriend, Armando, who held a canvas bag with glass bottles in his hand. Isabel let them in and they followed her to the kitchen.

"I'll warm the oven." Isabel turned the knob and slid the stone slab inside.

It was Armando's first time at the apartment. He sat on the sofa and clicked the TV on low volume.

Isabel didn't know him very well but, from Cristina's comments, he seemed like a nice guy.

Cristina placed the bottles in the refrigerator. "I hope you don't mind, we brought a bottle of dry white wine along with the sparkling water and the Sumol."

Isabel wiped her hands on the apron. "As long as you take the leftovers with you."

"If there are any, we will." Cristina gestured to her boyfriend. "Mando wanted to bring two bottles so I told him you don't like drinking."

The doorbell rang. Isabel raised her head from spreading the white garlic sauce on the surface of the first pizza. "I'm not expecting anyone else." She rarely had anyone knocking this late in the evening.

Cristina rose from the bar stool at the counter. "Oh, I forgot to tell you. I invited Simon Ackerley to join us for pizza night."

Isabel stilled. "You did what?"

"You left early, and I saw him in his office all alone. I asked him what he was doing tonight and he said nothing, so I gave him your address and told him to come."

Cristina walked out the kitchen door and Isabel jogged after her. "Why would you do that? You know I don't like him."

If she were being honest with herself, that wasn't entirely true.

"You don't mean that, Isabel. We both know it. I've seen the way you look at him." Cristina reached for the door handle.

"What do you mean, the way I look at him?"

Cristina ignored her.

This was not happening. Isabel took a deep breath. "He's after my job, you know that. That pretty much makes him my enemy." Maybe enemy was a strong word but that didn't mean he had to come over.

They stopped when the bell rang a second time. Isabel leaned against the peephole. The red hair. It was him, indeed.

Cristina glared at her. "Well, he's on the other side of this door. If you don't want him here, you tell him that." Then she walked toward the living room.

At least he didn't speak Portuguese, or he would have heard the whole conversation. He wasn't even inside yet and already it was awkward.

She unlocked the door and opened it. "Mr. Ackerley." He quirked an eyebrow at her. "I mean, Simon. Hi." She brightened her voice, hopefully not so much that it sounded fake. "Sorry for the wait."

He still wore the same pants, but his sleeves were rolled up to his elbows and he'd lost the necktie. How was it possible that he looked even better than earlier in the day? His hair was styled messily, like he'd raked his fingers through it too many times, which worked well for him. Isabel clung to the side of the door.

Simon Ackerley in her home. How was this happening? And why did she feel so nervous about it? She definitely didn't want to think about this now; she'd save it for later.

93

He smiled at her. "You did know I was coming, right? Cristina Fonseca invited me over."

Isabel returned the smile. How could she not? It was the first time she saw something akin to insecurity in his eyes. She knew the feeling all too well. "Yes, of course. Come on in, we're just getting started."

He followed her to the kitchen.

"You already know Cristina and that's her boyfriend, Armando."

Cristina stood at the counter, separating the sliced onions into rings, and Armando waved from the sofa.

Simon help a hand up to them. Then he turned to Isabel and handed her a box. "Here, you might want to put this in the freezer for later."

Isabel took it from him and put it away. "You didn't have to, but thank you." She took over from Cristina and finished arranging the rest of the toppings for the first pizza.

Cristina washed her hands at the sink. "My boyfriend's English is not very good, so I'm sorry if we seem to exclude you from our conversations. We're not being rude on purpose." She walked to the sofa and sat next to him.

Simon smiled. "It's fine, don't worry about me. I never say no to a home-cooked meal, so I hope you don't mind me coming."

Cristina cocked her head at Isabel and gave her a pointed look. Even without words, Isabel knew what she was trying to convey from across the room. Isabel wanted to roll her eyes. Yes, he was nervous, she could see that herself. And no, he wasn't that adorable. Puppies were adorable, not grown men with messy red hair.

Isabel worked on the pizzas. After a moment, Simon took the stool and sat by the counter. "So I'm guessing you got your oven repaired."

The timer beeped, and Isabel carefully transferred the pizzas onto the hot surface, side by side but with room to expand. She closed the oven and turned back to the counter. He remembered their conversation at the academy's kitchen. "Yes, thank goodness. I was beginning to have withdrawals."

He leaned his elbows on the granite surface and glanced at the pizzas lined up and awaiting their turn. "Not pepperoni?"

"Sorry to disappoint you, but pepperoni is not on the menu tonight."

"I'm curious, but definitely not disappointed." A crooked grin tugged at his lips.

He had a large mouth with full lips. On anyone else it would have looked out of proportion, but not on his face. It fit well with the straight nose, the green eyes, and the myriad freckles. She looked down at his arms. Strong arms with russet hair and more freckles.

Simon cleared his throat and Isabel grabbed a bowl from the counter. He'd caught her staring at him. Again. He was supposed to be the one feeling uncomfortable, not her.

"What kind of pizzas are you making?" he asked. The pizzas. Right.

Isabel turned the water on the dishes in the sink and cleaned the granite counter surface. "Three different ones. A spicy honey and caramelized onion with Portuguese cured ham, fresh cheese and arugula on a traditional crust. The second one is shrimp, black olives, and mango on a whole wheat crust, and the last one is a simple version of the classic margherita with fresh mozzarella, basil, and purple heirloom tomatoes."

It was his turn to stare back. "You had me at caramelized onions. Wow."

Isabel shrugged. "Don't be impressed yet. A couple of them are experiments and I'm trying out a white garlic sauce instead of a traditional tomato sauce for the base." She knew better than trying experiments on dinner guests, but she hadn't had the time to test the recipes first.

He glanced back at Cristina and Armando and lowered his voice. "If these pizzas are anything like the chocolate soufflés you made at the academy's kitchen, I'm sure they'll be amazing. I still dream about those soufflés, you know. And the madeleines you brought to the book club."

"How did you know I made those?"

"The Hargreaves told me. The orange flavor was so intriguing. Subtle, yet lingering."

The look in his eyes was captivating and she leaned in from her side of the counter. "I'll tell you the secret."

He leaned in as well. "What is it?"

"In addition to the orange zest, I also use a splash of water of orange blossom."

His eyes flashed. "Water of orange blossom?" he repeated in a reverent tone.

"It's water infused with fresh orange blossoms. Very simple but I use it sparingly or it can turn the dessert too perfumed."

Simon stared at her, smiling. "You're amazing, you know that? You run a private school by day and make the most delicious, beautiful food at night." His eyes crinkled at the corners. "Like I said, super powers."

Her cheeks heated. Darn compliments. She did not have any super powers.

Isabel tried to shrug it off but the admiration in his warm gaze was hard to ignore. She grabbed the edge of her apron and fanned the air around her. "Excuse me, could you open that door to the balcony behind you? It's getting a little hot in here with the oven on."

It was only the oven working too well, nothing else.

༄

Simon opened the glass sliding door and the breeze blew the curtains. Isabel's cheeks were flushed but whether it was the oven or his compliment he couldn't tell. He'd noticed how she always blushed when he complimented her, and he didn't mean to make her feel embarrassed. How could he have kept his appreciation for what she did to himself?

She'd changed from the conservative pantsuit and sensible heels she wore at the academy into cropped skinny jeans and bare feet. Her T-shirt was light blue with white letters proclaiming *It's a kale thing*, and at her waist she wore a ruffled apron in a floral print.

Isabel Antunes was a contradiction, a very interesting, very attractive one. The more he got to know her, the more he wanted to become her friend. Not a casual friend but a true one. She didn't trust easily and he understood why. Their relationship at work was delicate, even though he had no intention of taking her job. As he'd suspected, her friend had extended the invitation without telling her. Even if he didn't understand Portuguese, he'd heard his name through the door to know that she was surprised to find out he'd come, but she'd covered it well when she'd let him in. His presence tonight was an attempt at forming a friendship with her. Simon had taken a risk in coming, but how could he pass up the opportunity to see her outside of the academy? More than anything, he wished for him and Isabel to have the same kind of relationship Elliot and Amélie already had, and that wouldn't happen with the few moments of passing her in the hallway at work.

The kitchen opened to the living room through a double-wide doorless opening. On the sofa, Cristina and her boyfriend sat too cozily in front of the TV, a bit too close for Simon's comfort. A tall bookshelf displayed tightly packed books and small frames with photos on the opposite wall, and he approached to peruse the book spines. When he found a Portuguese edition of Sherlock Holmes, Simon pulled the first volume out and held it out to her. "Are you a Sherlock fan?"

Isabel looked up from her task. "A friend of mine recommended it."

"I grew up reading these stories."

She paused to look at him. Her eyebrows wrinkled, but she didn't reply.

Simon turned to replace the book on the shelf and hide a grin from her. He hadn't planned the slip up about something Elliot had told her, but maybe he could start dropping little hints. His time was running out soon, and he couldn't count on asking for an extension past the new year.

He went to help Isabel set the table placed between the counter and the sofa. "You didn't come to the book club on Sunday."

She arched an eyebrow, and he had to agree. His words hadn't come out as casually as he'd intended.

"Just curious, that's all," he added. They weren't at the point in their friendship where he could ask after her whereabouts.

She turned off the oven. "I was there early to drop off some baked goodies."

"The walnut muffins. You made those, didn't you?"

She nodded. "My grandmother's favorite recipe. But then I had to wash my hair."

He eyed her shoulder length hair. "How long can it really take?"

"I bet you don't know about deep conditioning treatments, do you?"

"Yes, I do. I do it once a month. The tap water in London is very hard." He kept a straight face.

Her lips twitched. "Then you know what a time commitment it is. We have the same problem in Lisbon."

Cristina stood from the sofa and gestured toward the television. She said something in Portuguese and motioned them to come closer. Simon walked to the sofa. It looked like an ad for a cooking show of some kind.

Isabel shook her head and replied to Cristina, but Cristina pulled at Isabel's hand until she sat between her and the boyfriend.

"Sorry for the drama. Cristina thinks I should enter this," Isabel said to him. When the ad was over, she returned to the kitchen.

Cristina turned to Simon. "Don't you think she should enter the competition?" She walked in the same direction. "You'd kill it, Isabel."

Isabel removed the pizzas from the oven and set them on the counter.

"What kind of competition is it?" Simon asked.

"It's an amateur chef competition," Isabel replied. "There's a preliminary audition and if you pass that, you go on the live TV show for two rounds. The first round starts out with twenty contestants who are voted off by viewers, and in the last round the four remaining contestants go face to face in front of a panel of professional chefs, food critics, and celebrities." She held a pizza wheel in her right hand. "As you see, no pressure at all."

Isabel called everyone to the table and he found himself seated across from her, the girls on one side and the guys on the other. In the center of the table, the pizzas were cut in squares and arranged on long rectangular white platters. A row of small white bowls with different colored sauces sat in between.

Simon waited for Isabel to say something since she was the hostess. Next to him, Cristina's boyfriend helped himself to the different pizzas and Cristina followed suit. Isabel caught Simon's eye and gave a small shrug. Her expression was soft and apologetic, and Simon nodded back at her in understanding.

When Cristina's boyfriend tried to fill Simon's glass from the bottle of white wine, Simon reached over to cover the glass.

"I don't drink," he said.

Isabel looked at him. "You don't?"

Cristina translated to her boyfriend and the guy smirked, but set the bottle down on the table.

Simon gazed at Isabel and shook his head slightly, hoping she understood he'd answer her questions later, if a chance arose. For now they lacked privacy, with Cristina and her boyfriend at the table with them.

Simon eyed a bottle of something that looked like soda.

"It's Sumol, Portuguese pineapple soda," Isabel said to him. He poured himself a drink.

Then she gestured at the bowls. "Those are dipping sauces: lemon-chive, honey with rosemary, and yogurt dill."

For a few minutes, they spooned the sauces onto their plates and tried the different pizzas, experimenting with combinations.

Simon slowed down and almost closed his eyes. "Wow," he said, looking at Isabel. "The lightness of the sauces with the texture of the crust and the rich flavors of the toppings—I don't know what to say."

All eyes turned to him. Isabel held his gaze and her cheeks pinked up, her eyes wide.

Cristina chuckled. "It sounds like you know what to say just fine. Do you understand now why I want Isabel to enter that competition? She'd be perfect."

"Truly, this is incredible." He took another bite.

"Plus, the prizes are fabulous," Cristina went on.

Isabel shook her head.

Cristina elbowed her. "Really? Tell him what the prizes are and see what he thinks." She jutted her chin toward Simon.

Isabel took the last piece of the arugula pizza onto her plate, then stood and placed the empty platter on the nearby counter. "The second prize is a six-month paid internship at the Tivoli resort, in southern Lisbon, across the river. They have the best chefs in the country." She sat down and pushed the last platter onto the center of the table. "And the first prize is twenty-five thousand euros in cash plus everything you need for the start-up of your own restaurant in downtown Lisbon."

Simon opened his mouth to reply, but Cristina's boyfriend asked Isabel a question as he reached into his pocket. She replied, shaking her head. Then he gestured at the balcony and said something, and Isabel said no again. Whatever it was, Cristina and the guy laughed it off awkwardly. When Isabel started clearing the table, Simon took the empty plates and followed her to the kitchen.

He joined Isabel at the sink as she filled it with water and soap.

She lowered her voice. "Sorry about that. Armando wanted to smoke and I told him no."

"And then he asked to smoke out in the balcony and you said no again," he said to her.

Isabel nodded. "Yes, I did." She drew her hands out of the suds and wiped them on her apron. "Smoking is so insidious. Apart from all the reasons why smoking is just not good for anyone, even being next to a smoker interferes with smell and taste. And I don't like that. Besides, the scent clings to the walls and furniture. It's just gross." Her cheeks colored. "You don't smoke do you?"

Simon shook his head. "I don't. I happen to feel the same as you about it."

Her posture relaxed. "Good. It barely occurred to me that maybe you smoked and I was going on about how much I hate it. I really didn't want to offend anyone."

"It's your home and your rules." Simon set the glasses by the sink. "They should respect that."

Cristina carried the last platter in. "Isabel, we hate to eat and run, but we're going." She turned to Simon. "Don't leave on our account, Simon. Stay and keep Isabel company."

Her boyfriend stood in the living room and waved goodbye. Isabel walked with them to the foyer and they all talked animatedly for a few moments before she closed the door behind them.

When she returned to the kitchen, he had his hands plunged in sudsy water, scrubbing one of the platters.

"It wasn't my plan to have you do the dishes, you know." She grabbed a clean dishcloth and started drying the ones on the rack.

Simon looked over her way and smiled. "After the dinner you served tonight, I'll gladly do the dishes every time." He paused. "Not that I'm trying to invite myself over again. But if you do, I mean, invite me, I don't mind washing." His neck heated. "I'll just stop now."

Isabel smiled. "How can I refuse that offer?"

Working together, they had the kitchen cleaned and everything put away in a few minutes. It surprised him, this side of Isabel. At the academy, she had a wall around her, always on edge every time he approached, as if waiting for him to say or do something against her.

But tonight she was relaxed. She looked younger, her expression was softer and more open, and Simon wanted to spend many more evenings like this one. It could even be a start for bringing up the subject of Elliot.

He had no doubts now. Isabel was Amélie. Despite his initial reluctance, he'd looked up Amélie's ISP signature. Combined with seeing his letter in Isabel's possession when she'd crashed onto his bicycle, and the strong feeling he'd experienced when they'd met his first day at the academy, there was nothing left to doubt. Now he just had to find the right time to tell her.

He leaned against the door jamb, searching for a reason to stay a little longer, wanting to prolong his time with her.

Isabel opened the freezer and reached for the box he'd brought earlier. "Let's see what you have in here." She looked inside and then back at him. "You're either very good at guessing or you had an inside tip."

Simon shrugged. "I asked Cristina if I should bring something tonight and she said if I wanted to impress you, I should get lemon gelato from the Tricolore gelataria."

"And you wanted to impress me?" She didn't smile, but her eyes were soft.

"Did I succeed?" Simon couldn't remember the last time he'd wanted to impress a woman this much.

Isabel set two white bowls on the counter. "I'm impressed you actually listened to her suggestion." She scooped out the frozen dessert evenly and held out a spoon to him. "I usually eat mine straight from the carton. But I don't want you to get the wrong impression."

She sat on the sofa, legs crossed. Simon followed her and sat at the other end. They ate in silence for a few minutes.

Simon licked the spoon with the last bite. "This ice cream is really good."

"It's gelato, not ice cream." She scraped at the bottom of the bowl. "There's a slight difference. Gelato usually has no eggs in the recipe and is churned slower, which makes it denser than ice cream. But you're right, it's really, really good."

"But not as good as your pizza. Where did you learn to cook like that?"

Her spoon clinked against the side of the bowl. "From my grandmother." She glanced at him with a sad smile on her lips. "The earliest memories I have are of me and Avó Marta in the kitchen. I was too little to reach the counter so she got a chair for me." Her eyes crinkled. "And the apron was so big."

"Ah, so that explains your apron collection," he said.

She raised her head. "When did you see my apron collection?"

He gestured towards the kitchen. "The pantry door was ajar. Impressive collection, by the way."

She nodded. "Avó Marta sewed the first ones for me."

"Sounds like you were really close."

Isabel put the spoon down and looked at him. "She was the one who raised me and we always did everything together." She paused.

Simon leaned forward. "I'm sorry, Isabel. I know the memories are hard." Couldn't he say something better than such trite words? Maybe he shouldn't have brought it up.

Isabel walked to the sink and placed her bowl inside. "They're bittersweet, you know? When I'm cooking, I feel closer to her. But those are also the moments when I miss her the most."

He was well acquainted with bittersweet memories. "I feel the same way when I read my mom's favorite books." He pulled out his phone and tapped on the screen until he found the picture he wanted. "This was our last summer together," he said, holding up the phone to Isabel.

"May I?" she asked.

Simon nodded and handed her the phone. She walked to the living room and sat on the sofa. After a brief hesitation, he joined her.

"Your mother was beautiful," she said, as she looked at his favorite picture of him and Mom on the beach.

He moved closer and extended his arm behind Isabel, pointing at the phone with his other hand.

"How old were you?"

"Almost fifteen in this picture."

"You look a lot like her," Isabel said, with a smile in her voice. "Your eyes and your nose. Not your hair color."

He chuckled. "No, that's all Dad, from his Scottish mother."

"You both look so happy."

"We were," Simon replied, his mind filling with the joyful memories he had of that time. "I was very close to my mom, being an only child."

Isabel rose her eyes from the phone to look at him. "We have that in common."

As he turned his attention to her, something changed between them, something soft and strong and brimming with a quiet sweetness. The need to hold her and kiss her lit a craving inside him and his eyes dipped to her mouth.

Was it his wishful thinking or did Isabel lean closer to him?

Whatever it was, it passed all too quickly.

She straightened and returned the phone to him. "Thank you for sharing that with me."

Reluctantly, Simon removed his arm from the back of the sofa and put some distance between them. "You're welcome. Thank you for indulging me."

When she disappeared down the hallway with a hasty excuse me, Simon stood and walked to the balcony.

The hour was late, the clear night loaded with an inky blackness of a moonless sky, dispelled only by the city lights.

Maybe he should leave.

When Isabel returned, he pulled away from the glass doors. "I think I should go." Before he did something dumb, like kiss her and tell her everything.

"Can I show you something before you leave?"

"Yes, of course."

In her hands, she carried an old-fashioned double frame, the kind with a hinge down the center and two panes on each side. She opened it wide and Simon held one pane while she grasped the other, exposing the photos inside.

"This is me with my parents, two months before their accident."

"You were the cutest toddler." Simon smiled at the photograph of her mother holding a very young Isabel and her father embracing them both. It was a moment of perfect happiness suspended in time, and he could almost guess that bittersweetness she'd mentioned earlier.

"And this one is of my Avó Marta and me a few years ago. It's my favorite picture of us."

Both she and her grandmother had their arms around each other, their cheeks touching, their smiles bright and full of love.

How did she feel looking at these? Did they make her happy or did she mourn for her lost family?

After spending a few more minutes with Isabel, as she related the story behind the photograph, Simon walked to the front door.

"Thank you for letting me crash your pizza night," he said, unable to rein in his smile.

She opened the door for him. "I'm glad you came. Consider it an open invitation from now on."

Her warm voice and genuine tone melted his heart. "I'll take you up on it."

"You should. I mean it."

Just as he extended his hand to shake hers, Isabel reached up for an air-kiss, her cheek touching his. They fumbled for an awkward instant and she stepped away from him, her face tinted with a blush.

His heart beat wildly in his chest, surprise and desire rising together within him.

"I'm sorry. I shouldn't have done that," she said, looking down. "Force of habit. Portuguese habit, I should say."

Simon took her hand and squeezed her fingers gently to get her attention. "No apologizing necessary, Isabel."

Before he lost his nerve, he bent and kissed her cheek, then left.

CHAPTER ELEVEN

To: ameliefaithfulfriend@mail.com
From: elliotbestpenpal@mail.com

Dear Amélie,
This morning the sky was blue. There's a nip in the air and the days are shorter. I haven't had to carry an umbrella yet, but I know it's coming. Until then, I'm determined to enjoy the sun in whatever form it comes.

My job is supposed to be like a 9-5 thing but that rarely happens. I don't get overtime when I stay over, but I'm getting compensated more than those around me, and that's not too fair to them or me. Too many misguided expectations on both sides, but let's not bring that up.

I'm sorry that your last boyfriend was a jerk, but I'm not sorry that he left you. You deserve better than a guy who treats you like he did, Amélie. Nobody *deserves to be in a relationship without mutual respect and apprecia-tion, not to mention friendship and love.*

*Oh, the joys of d*ating. I could tell you some stories. The last time I went on a date, I let my dad convince me to meet this young woman who was the daughter of an acquaintance of his. We'd attended the same uni and apparently that was enough in common to deem us com-patible. Yeah, I know, a blind date— we were doomed before we met. The bigger problem was that she was still attending the same uni I had ten years prior. She was only nineteen, a little detail nobody thought to mention. She looked even younger, and here I was at my old age, taking her for a night out. I kept looking over my shoulder for someone to stop and accuse me of leading a minor astray. It couldn't have been more awkward if we'd planned it.

I'm afraid the girlfriend I had before that didn't end on a happy note either. What did I tell you? I'm not good at relationships.

And what does it say about me that I want to try again? Actually, I'd like my next girlfriend to be my last one. I'm ready to move on, ready for what comes after the dating.

Always your friend,
Elliot

P.S.—I attached a picture of the little bird who's been visiting the window sill in my bedroom. I leave him bread crumbs and he leaves me—definitely not bread crumbs.

༼ ༽

To: elliotbestpenpal@mail.com
From: ameliefaithfulfriend@mail.com

Dear Elliot,
I looked up that little bird on the internet (blessed Google) and it is indigenous to Western Europe. That narrows down a little your possible locations. Keep sending clues. ;)

I've never had problems with being lonely before, but lately I find myself yearning to be an important part of someone's life. This feeling catches me by surprise, sometimes when I'm taking a walk and see couples holding hands, or when I go to the movies and see a man place his arm around a woman's shoulders. I feel like I'm a half of a magnet, pushing and pulling at everyone else around me, and not finding the other half that completes me. I'm not making much sense, I know.

Not too far from where I live there's a belvedere with magnificent views of the city, and it's been a favorite spot to go since I was a young girl. Sometimes I go there and sit for a while, imagining I have someone sitting beside me. That's my pathetic life.

There's something my friend wants me to do. She won't stop nagging me about it. I told her it's not for me but she insists it is. I'll tell you a secret, Elliot: I really want to do this. I've been dreaming about this for a long, long time, and I know I can do it. But I'm scared because there are others who are better than me, and who am I to try it out if I'm not the best at it? So I stay awake at night thinking about it, but in the morning I still don't do anything about it.

Well, that was a bit too personal. Sometimes I write these emails to you without a second reading otherwise I'd delete them. And there I go again into something I shouldn't. Let's get back to a safe topic, like the weather.

I think the crisp autumn weather is here to stay. Some of the shops downtown have started working on their Christmas displays, which is a little too early, if you ask me. I don't like to think about it until December 1st.

What are your plans for Christmas? Are you going back to London to spend the holiday with your family?

Faithfully,
Amélie

Chapter Twelve

Simon pushed the door open to his office and set the tablet on the desk. Only thirty minutes left for the last bell of the day, and he was ready for the weekend. The work was progressing on target, and he would be able to deliver the full reports before the academy closed for the Christmas holiday, as he'd planned. As for the online portal, he only had a few minor updates and he'd have it running before the end of the month. He was also on the verge of figuring out how to attach a tracker to the signature of the security card that had been used to access the academy's portal, the one swiped from Isabel to do the money transfers. If only he could confide in her and share his progress.

Unfortunately, Isabel still didn't trust him at work. When he'd had dinner at her apartment, she'd been different, more relaxed and open, and the way she'd said goodbye before he left had been a pleasant surprise. That easiness between them—he wanted it back and he wanted more of it. He had to get her away from the academy and from the atmosphere that had her thinking he was against her. If only for a few hours, he had to try and deepen their friendship.

When the bell rang, Simon went out in the front courtyard as the students left for the day. Isabel stood by the gate, talking to the children and some of their parents. After the last pick up and the last goodbyes, Isabel went inside and he followed her to her office.

The door was ajar and he knocked on the jamb. "How was your day?"

Isabel raised her head from her tablet and blew out a long breath. "I haven't been this excited for a Friday since..."

"Last week?" he offered.

"At least." She paused and smiled at him.

She had a small dimple on her right cheek when she smiled. How had he not noticed it before?

"I can't believe this is only first term," she went on. "It feels so busy already."

"I'm partially responsible for that, with all the changes we've introduced so far." His presence at the academy had only added to the pressure of her job, but in the long run, it would make the work lighter for her and everyone else at the small school.

Isabel raised an eyebrow but didn't comment as she resumed her note taking.

Simon lingered for a moment. What else could he say that wouldn't sound lame?

"Any plans for the weekend?" Isabel asked. She turned off the tablet and stowed it in a drawer, locking it.

"Yes, grocery shopping. And then it will be me and some frozen Italian dinners and catching up on reading."

"Frozen dinners?" She looked pointedly at him. "Why can't you cook dinner the old-fashioned way?"

"It would be great if I could cook even half of what you can, but alas, it's a talent I don't have."

She waved a hand and frowned at him. "That's an excuse if I ever heard one. Anyone can cook."

Simon straightened. "I beg to differ. Anyone can not." He stressed the last word.

Isabel came around the desk and stood in front of him. "Yes, you can."

Her expression was firm, but her eyes belied the humor behind the words. "You said Italian, didn't you?"

She turned to her desk and ripped a page from a paper pad. She scribbled for a few moments then handed him the scrap of paper. "You're cooking tonight, at my place. Go to the store and buy these ingredients, then come over. I've got the rest of the ingredients that you'll need to make the best meal you've ever cooked."

There was a hint of challenge in her brown eyes, vivid and warm.

"You're not giving me much of a choice, are you?"

Disappointment flickered in her gaze but she quickly disguised it. "Of course it's your choice. Just know it's a one-time offer."

He scanned the list. "Give me forty minutes and I'll be there."

She let him pass first then locked the office door. "Take an hour if you have to. Friday evening grocery shopping is not for the faint of heart."

An hour later, Simon arrived at Isabel's apartment, his hands loaded with bags. She'd been right, of course. The store had been busy, but he'd been focused on buying what was on the list and leaving as quickly as possible.

Isabel opened the door with a bright smile and a checkered apron around her waist. Her T-shirt read *My spoon is bigger than yours* with the image of a wooden spoon running below. She wore her hair coiled on top of her head.

"I was beginning to think you'd changed your mind." She waved him in and took a bag. "Any problems?"

Simon followed her to the kitchen. "Nothing that I couldn't find an answer to on Google."

"Next time, send me a text. I'm not sure I can recommend Google for this kind of activity."

When he'd started at the academy, she'd made a point of letting him know he could email her after hours but she didn't want any other form of communication. "I don't have your personal number, remember?"

She emptied the contents of the bags onto the counter. "We can remedy that easily. Remind me before you leave."

Simon resisted the urge to grab his phone and add her number that very moment. "I will."

For a few minutes, they busied themselves sorting the ingredients into categories.

Isabel handed him a black apron with a border of red hearts. "This is the manliest apron I own."

Simon took it from her and tied it on. "Not a problem."

"The first thing you need to do is brown the beef." She placed a wide pan on the stove. "This is a sauté pan."

He peeled back the butcher paper and dumped the beef in the pan.

"There's an open house and lecture on American literature in the early twentieth century at the book-store and organized by the university. It's open to the public." Simon stirred the beef. "Would you be interested in going?"

"I don't think so. The whole premise behind these activities sounds suspicious to me." She leaned against the counter for a moment. "Everybody there has ulterior motives."

"It might not be as bad as you think. And some-times it's fun to meet new people."

Isabel laughed. "If you could see your face as you said that. I'm sure you have the same expression when you're telling someone about going to the dentist."

She lowered the pitch of her voice. "Oh, it's not so bad getting my teeth pulled."

"I sound nothing like that." Her impression wasn't very good and Simon smiled. It was impossible to keep a straight face when she was teasing him and looking so adorable doing so. "I don't even have a British accent."

Isabel placed a package of spaghetti on the counter. "You don't sound like a Yankee either. How does an American end up in England anyway?" She eyed the onion on the cutting board. "Don't stop chopping. You can chop and talk at the same time, you know. And don't forget the beef."

"Yes, Chef." He chopped too slowly, but Isabel waited until he was done.

"Let's drain the beef and put it aside," she said.

Simon followed her instructions and then she showed him how to smash a few garlic heads which he added to the same large pan with the onions and olive oil. "Okay, pay attention now. This is called a *refogado*. It's the base for most stews, soups, rice, anything else considered good cooking." She gave it a quick stir and then handed the wooden spoon to him. "Don't let the onions burn, we just want them to sweat."

"Which is…" Simon took the spoon and stirred.

"We only want the onions cooked through and translucent without crisping the garlic. Then you can add back the browned beef and some seasoning."

Simon poured the beef in the pan. "This is a lot to keep up with."

"You're doing fine, Simon Ackerley." She handed him a can of tomatoes which already had the lid removed. "Stop overthinking it. Cooking is supposed to be intuitive."

He added the tomatoes to the pan. "Why the canned tomatoes instead of the fresh ones?"

"This time of year, the fresh tomatoes are from a hothouse and they lack flavor. So tell me, how did you end up in England?" She repeated the question.

"My father is English and he met my mother at Boston University." He looked at her. "She was actually from New York but went to Massachusetts to study in Social Sciences." Simon paused, as his mind went through the photos in the big album that sat in the library at home, the ones Mom had patiently told him about over and over when he was little. "After my mom died, Dad decided to return to London."

"So is it just you and your dad? Do you have any siblings?" she asked.

"No siblings. My mom said I was her miracle baby." Simon gave the pan a stir. "Mom was an only child and Dad has a brother just outside of London, so it just made sense to move back to the old country."

"Was it very hard?" Isabel asked.

Very hard? How could he tell her about it? About the people he didn't understand despite knowing they spoke the same language he did, the strange food and stranger habits? Or the kids who whispered behind his back? And all of it while missing his mother fiercely, and knowing he probably wouldn't go back to the United States for a long, long time, if ever.

He shrugged. "It could have been worse. I got through it eventually."

"There you go, being all optimistic about it. Even so, it must have been difficult for you." She glanced at him as she went through the spices in the cabinet. "How about school? How did you manage that?"

He winced a little. "School proved harder than we'd thought. We moved in the middle of the school year so I finished those few months at home and then started the ninth grade in the fall instead of moving up to the tenth."

"As if you didn't have enough going on." She handed him a small jar of dried oregano. "I hope at least you made some new friends."

Simon nodded. "I was lucky I did." Blessed, really. "I met a friend in ninth grade and that helped me a lot, to have someone to talk to." The best friend he ever had.

Isabel held his gaze for a little while, and the understanding in her eyes almost matched all the things he wished he could tell her. What would she say if she knew how much he valued Amélie's friendship?

"Come on, it's time to make the salad." She brightened. "You've made salad before, right?"

"I'm going to assume you mean something more than opening a bag of pre-washed lettuce and greens?"

She rolled her eyes. "Simon Ackerley, how did you get to the ripe old age of thirty without knowing how to prepare a salad?"

Isabel also showed him how to cook and drain the spaghetti, to which he added the meat and sauce in a serving bowl. She had set the table earlier and, as she approached the chair to sit, Simon held it out for her. He paused for a moment, staring at the back of her neck and the unobstructed view of the trail of stars imprinted there. His fingers itched to reach and touch the graceful curve, and he patted the sides of the chair instead.

Isabel turned around to face him. "What's the matter?"

"Your tattoo. What does it mean?"

She brushed at it. "It's an interpretation of the north star. Stars, I should say. It has a tail. Just a reminder to look up and find my direction. Avó Marta said something to me once and it gave me the idea." She brushed the back of her neck, and his fingers itched to do the same.

"You don't like it?" she asked looking over her shoulder at him.

"No, nothing like that." He liked it too much, and had the urge to bend down and kiss her there. He rounded the table and took a seat. "I think it's pretty."

"Go ahead, try it," Isabel urged him.

Simon picked up his fork and took a bite. The flavors amazed him. "Wow, this is really good," he said. "What do you call this dish?"

"It's like a Portuguese version of spaghetti a la Bolognese, and you'll find as many versions as there are cooks, since everyone likes to add their own touch. As you get more confident, you'll start doing the same."

"I'm not sure I'm brave enough for that."

"Of course you are." Isabel smiled wide. "Didn't I say you could cook?"

"Only because of you." The tone of his voice surprised him. He hadn't meant to sound so serious.

Could she feel it, this sense of gratitude that washed over him, the warmth that infused his chest? Whatever he'd accomplished tonight was thanks to her. Simon put down his fork and reached for her left hand. The moment his fingers touched her skin, the contact electrified him. It shot up his arm and straight to his chest. His hand rested on hers, and he didn't know what to do next. Would it always be like this, an ordinary touch that was nothing but?

Isabel stilled, her eyes wide. The fork lay forgotten at the edge of the plate. The smile on her lips wavered a bit, but she didn't move her hand.

She had felt it. Whatever this was between them, she had felt it too.

"If cooking means so much to you, you should come for another lesson." She pressed his fingers before releasing them then met his eyes. Though she hadn't voiced her words as a question, the uncertainty and doubt were there.

"If you'll have me again, I'll be here," he replied a bit more gravely than he'd intended.

She nodded. "Of course."

He nodded back, grinning at her in a ridiculous fashion. "Good."

Isabel picked up her glass and took a drink of water. "What kind of food do you like? Other than Italian."

"A nice plate of roast beef and seasoned potatoes," he said. "My father's favorite. Growing up, we always went to the pub on the corner for Sunday lunch."

From there the conversation easily moved to the merits of Portuguese cuisine over English cooking, how daily fresh bread was the food of the gods, and how nothing else compared to a slice of homemade flan pudding.

"I'll take your word for it about the pudding," he said. "I've never had the pleasure of trying home-made flan."

Isabel shook her head. "Your lack of culinary diversity is quite amazing. But considering you lived in America and then moved to England, I shouldn't be so surprised."

Simon raised an eyebrow, a smile twitching his lips. "Before I came to Portugal, I'd have been offended at that remark, but you're quite spoiling my palate and I couldn't be happier for that."

She met his gaze, her eyes bright and smiling. "What will you do with yourself when you return to England, Simon Ackerley?"

"I'll miss your cooking something fierce," he admitted.

He couldn't even think how much more he would miss her. How could he entertain not seeing her every day?

❦

Isabel watched from her balcony as Simon turned the corner down the street and walked away from her building. Hopefully he didn't have to walk too far.

What an enjoyable evening her time with him turned out to be. Inviting him over had been unplanned, a spur of the moment idea she hadn't been too sure about. But Simon had taken to her suggestion of a cooking lesson and followed all her instructions, and they'd had the most fun.

Her phone rang, interrupting her thoughts. Isabel retrieved it from her purse and swiped at the screen, telling herself she didn't wish it could be Simon who'd forgotten to tell her something.

It was Jacinta. After a brief hesitation, Isabel answered the phone and greeted her cousin.

"Isabel, I'm so glad I caught you. Is this a bad time? It's not too late, is it?"

"Not too late at all. I'm glad you called. I had a friend over for dinner earlier and he just barely left. Sorry I didn't answer last time."

"Hang on. You had a guy over for dinner?" Jacinta asked.

"It's not like that," Isabel said. "He only came for a cooking lesson."

"Sure he did."

Jacinta had always manged to be unassuming and curious at the same time. "It was nothing more than that, I assure you. His name is Simon Ackerley."

"Simon Ackerley?" Jacinta repeated, a clear interest in her voice. "Is he American?"

"An American who lives in London. He was hired to work on the academy's online platform as a temporary consultant."

"So you see him every day."

"Pretty much, yes. The academy is not that large of a place."

"Simon sounds promising," Jacinta said in a sing-song tone.

"Just because you married an American doesn't mean all your cousins will too."

Jacinta laughed. "Knox, do you know what Isabel just said?" She repeated Isabel's words to her husband and laughed again.

"What's so funny?" Isabel asked.

"I have three of my Romano cousins who have married Americans, and there's another one who's about to do the same."

"I'm not a Romano," Isabel said.

"No, but you're my cousin."

CHAPTER THIRTEEN

*I*sabel turned in bed. The chink of light through the window tiptoed across the opposite wall. Mornings were lazy coming in as winter approached. Was it Friday or Saturday?

The memories from Friday night rushed in. Simon in the kitchen. Simon cooking dinner. Simon laughing and listening to her. They'd talked and they'd had fun and they'd worked together.

And then she'd air-kissed him at the door.

He'd returned the gesture but with a real kiss on her cheek. She could almost still feel his lips on her skin.

The invitation for the cooking lesson at her apartment had come almost as a challenge. When he'd hesitated, Isabel hid the disappointment quickly. But he'd changed his mind, and she was glad for it. They'd started out the evening simply cooking, like it had been her plan, working side by side and enjoying each other's company. As the evening wore on, something between them changed, first holding hands at the table, sitting close to each other on the sofa, his arm casually over the back and almost touching her shoulders. By the time he walked to the door, she just brushed his cheek with hers, not even thinking about what she was doing.

How could something so simple carry so much heat, so much meaning? Just the memory of his hand on top of hers raised gooseflesh up her arm. Her cheeks heated and Isabel blew out a slow breath.

She hadn't expected this connection to Simon. The more she got to know him, the more she realized he was nothing like her first impression.

Why couldn't their relationship be this easy at work? She wasn't proud of the cold way she treated him at the academy. He was only doing his job, which was making things better for the faculty and students. But somehow she was unable to lower her defenses and it usually ended up showing in her behavior or in her words toward him.

The book club was the neutral ground, the place where they treated each other as if nothing ever happened at work to put them at odds. Herself at odds with him, to be honest. Simon was always smiling and in a good mood, never at odds with anybody, least of all her.

In the beginning, she hadn't wanted to sit by him at the upper floor of The Queen's English, as not to give the wrong impression—to whom, she really didn't know, but that didn't matter anymore. They were some sort of friends, right? Friends could sit by each other without people assuming there was more to it, couldn't they? She'd seen Mary Hargreaves glance at them and Isabel could easily guess what the older lady speculated, but so far Mary hadn't made any comments.

Simon was an attractive man, one of the few in her circle, and those who knew her also knew she hadn't dated in a while. With the russet hair and green eyes of his, with the way he cut a figure in the well-tailored dark gray suit, or in shirt sleeves and a neck tie, Simon stood out, whether he meant to or not. And she'd notice him. Every day a little more, she noticed something different about him.

Isabel didn't want the fragile relationship between them to become more complicated. They'd both felt the connection on Friday at her apartment; there had been too many signs to ignore it. She'd feared he'd bring it up later, but he hadn't.

Instead, Isabel had agreed to accompany him to the open house at the bookstore. A misplaced sense of duty, something she was not ready to fully analyze. Friends did things with friends. It was as simple as that, wasn't it?

How awkward would it be when they saw each other outside of work? At least at the academy they were bound by duty to act professionally, something that came with its own safety.

Isabel took a breath and chided herself. She was over-thinking it.

By the time Simon rang the bell to pick her up, she had changed outfits three times. Not that it mattered. She was only going out with a friend.

Deep breath.

She swung the door open and Simon greeted her with a wide smile. Isabel grabbed the door jamb. It wasn't fair the way her heart sped up a little at that smile, at the sight of the man in front of her.

Only friends. Nothing more than friends.

"You look great, Isabel," he said.

"Thank you." Simon did too but she couldn't get the words out. The dark jeans, the brown blazer and a rust colored pullover gave him a casual look he didn't wear too often, and she liked it.

When they reached the street outside, Simon pulled out his phone. "I should have called a taxi already."

"No, don't call. I'll show you how fun the Lisbon underground can be." Isabel argued the benefits of taking the Metro instead as they walked to the nearest station.

The afternoon was warm for the season, a late summer kind of day instead of late fall, with a soft breeze blowing in from the river and playing with the brightly colored leaves on the sidewalks. Isabel guided Simon in and out of underground stations, surfacing at streets where she could show him something typical and picturesque of the city. It was the kind of day to be spent outside, not at lecture. As much as she liked books, lectures were not her favorite. Maybe she could convince Simon to do something else, instead.

They walked from the last station, just around the corner from the bookstore.

Isabel checked the time. It had started thirty minutes ago. "I think I made us late. I'm sorry."

Simon looked in her direction. "Don't be. That was the most fun underground ride I've taken in ages."

When they arrived at the main door, Isabel stopped and turned to Simon. "Do you know how long it's supposed to go on?"

"I don't, but I guess we're about to find out."

A few people stood downstairs in small groups. Some turned to look at Simon and Isabel, but she didn't recognize any of the book club members. Why had she come at all?

Simon stepped closer to her. His arm brushed hers and he took her hand. A rush of heat crept up Isabel's neck and her breath stopped short. She looked up at him and he squeezed her fingers gently, a small smile forming at the corners of his mouth.

He leaned in her direction and lowered his voice. "Let's see how this goes."

She nodded, unable to think of a reply as she tried to deal with the reaction to his proximity. What did he mean by it? Did he want people to think they were together? Technically, they were since they'd come together. But that was only it, wasn't it?

The lecture had already finished and people trickled down the stairs where an exhibit and book signing were about to take place. Despite the ample space, having more people than usual milling around made the store feel smaller and more crowded than it really was.

"Who knew early American literature was so popular?" she said.

"It's the call of the wild," Simon said with a small chuckle.

She smiled at the joke. "Emphasis on wild, from the way the store looks tonight."

Mary waved from behind the counter. "How is my favorite couple today?"

Couple? What did she mean by that?

Isabel's chest squeezed and her eyes dropped to Simon's hand holding hers, the awareness rushing to the feel of his skin, to the pleasing weight of his fingers against her own.

He followed her gaze to her hand and then spoke to Mary. "How are you, Mary? This place is hopping today."

Mary said something but Isabel couldn't concentrate on her words. Between the din of the people talking and the sound of her blood in her ears, the loudness amplified Isabel's thoughts.

She let go of Simon's hand and stepped back. "I'll wait outside for you."

Once on the street, Isabel breathed in deeply, then started walking to the corner.

She'd left without waiting for his reply. But her reaction to Mary's comment had taken her by surprise. Why did it bother her that Mary Hargreaves thought she and Simon were a couple?

Or was it because they weren't a couple?

Isabel let the honesty of that notion sink more consciously into her understanding. Was there any question to her confusion, the way her feelings ran too hot and too cold, not really knowing how she felt about Simon? The fact he was only in Lisbon because he'd been hired to work at the academy still bothered her more than she wanted, especially as she'd found him to be so different than the person she'd believed him to be in the beginning.

But deep down the truth had a way of niggling at her and she couldn't think of Simon without thinking of Elliot. How realistic was it that she didn't even know the real name of the man who held her heart?

By the time Isabel walked back to the bookstore, Simon stood by the door with a college-age young woman who was smiling too much.

He said something and the girl laughed, then flipped her long hair over her shoulder. Classic flirting behavior. Next she would be leaning toward him and touching his arm or shoulder.

His forearm. She actually touched his forearm as she doubled over laughing. Clearly putting on a show to impress him.

Isabel hid her annoyance. Why did she view overly happy people as fake? Not all of them, of course, but some definitely pushed it, like this girl did.

When Simon caught sight of Isabel, his expression brightened. Was he really happy to see her? Her face softened and she smiled back at him.

As she approached them, she heard the girl asking Simon a question.

"… like to come?"

Isabel stepped close to Simon, brushing his arm with hers. "Actually, we can't stay. But thanks for the offer."

Simon said goodbye to the girl and followed until he took hold of Isabel's hand. "Wait for me, please."

She turned "Do you want to stay? I don't want to, but you can go back and accept her invitation, if you want."

Simon arched a brow at her. "If you don't want to stay, I'm not staying either. And I don't want to go to a poetry slam at the university café either."

"Is that what she invited you to?"

He held her gaze. "It's you I want to spend time with, Isabel."

Well, she hadn't asked, but Simon had let her know without any room for doubts. He wanted to be with her, at least for today. She wouldn't think of the future for now.

They resumed walking side by side, holding hands as if they'd done it plenty of times before, as if they spent time every day like this. When was the last time she went walking with a guy? She couldn't even remember. Her pulse beat fast and her breath hitched in her chest, all because Simon Ackerley held her hand.

Isabel looked down the street and spotted a cable car ascending slowly from the other side. She turned to Simon and smiled. "Have you been down by the river yet?"

๛

Simon glanced at their joined hands. How he loved to hold her hand. Whatever she had in mind, he'd do it. If it took a long time, even better.

"No, I haven't been by the river yet," he replied.

He'd taken some bike rides in the areas around the rented apartment and the academy, but other than a few gardens in between, he hadn't had the time to go exploring much. This chance to see Lisbon through Isabel's eyes was what he'd been hoping for.

Isabel tugged him toward the tram stop and checked the route on the posted schedule. "We'll have to switch cars halfway through the ride." Again, her expression brightened. "We'll take the elétrico and stop downtown."

They climbed aboard when the yellow tram came to a stop and once inside Isabel dropped the euro coins to pay for the fare before he realized what she'd done.

She found a seat by the window and Simon sat beside her. "The ride back is on me." He reached for her hand again, and this time she squeezed back his fingers.

"So this is what you call the electric?" The tram they rode in was a modern one made to resemble the style of the older ones he'd seen in postcards and brochures of the city.

She gestured toward the outside of the car. "On account of the electric wires above."

It was an unhurried ride, clanging along the metal tracks and stopping every so often to board other passengers also enjoying the autumn afternoon. They got off and switched to another line and a different tram car, this time a genuine antique one carefully restored with gleaming brass fixtures and polished wood. Along the way, Isabel pointed out the neighborhoods, or bairros, the downtown shops, and the monuments he hadn't had the time to explore yet.

But for everything the city had to offer, it was her Simon wanted to see. Isabel had her hair down today. She always wore it coiled at the nape of her neck during the week and Simon liked the way it looked, just barely past her shoulders. The red sweater brightened her expression and even her chocolate eyes seemed lighter and less stressed. This was the Isabel he'd been wanting to spend time with, relaxed and unworried, sitting beside him like a friend, and maybe even something more.

As the tram passed from a narrow street onto an open square, Isabel stood and pulled him along. "Come on. This is our stop."

Before them, the square extended twice as long and wide as a football field, paved in a crisscross of white stones with a statue of a military man on a horse in its center. At the far end, an open dock flanked by stone pillars opened to the river, and to the right, the river Tagus gave way to the Atlantic Ocean, the bridge serving as a gate to the expanse beyond.

After crossing the square, they sat on the stone benches by the dock.

"You know, with all the similarities between Lisbon and London, the two cities are so different," he said.

The breeze tossed her hair behind her and she turned to face the river. "I spent a day in London, once."

Simon stilled. She'd been in London and he'd never known about it. "How long ago was that?"

"About ten years ago, maybe a little more. It was a quick trip with some friends from college, three days in Paris and a little stop in London over the spring holiday."

He'd been in Boston then, visiting all the places where his mother had grown up, where his parents had met. Isabel had never said anything about her trip to London. Well, Amélie hadn't mentioned it, and he couldn't ask Isabel why.

"You'll have to come back when you have more time and I'll give you a tour of my favorite spots." He squeezed her hand and she turned to look at him, the lopsided dimple flashing at him. The urge to kiss her welled in his chest and its intensity took Simon by surprise. But this was not the moment.

A church bell nearby clanged the approaching evening hour and Isabel paused. "I don't know about you, but I'm famished and could have some dinner. What about some local gastronomy?" she asked. "What have you tried so far?"

"I'm afraid not much," he confessed. "I don't mind trying new foods but the language barrier could be a problem and then I'd have to eat some weird things I'd rather avoid."

"I know a little restaurant not too far from here," she said. "I promise you won't have to eat anything you don't want to."

"Lead the way then," he told her.

A breeze lifted from the river and they set out walking back toward the streets. After a few minutes, they caught another tram that climbed a few streets back into the city, until they got off and walked the rest of the way, amid the early twinkle of lights.

Isabel took him to a little restaurant tucked on a side street away from the busy areas where tourists milled.

A few patrons were seated near the front but they were led to a square table at the back, in a more private corner, much to Simon's gladness. He pulled up a chair for Isabel and sat to her right instead of across from her.

She said a few words to the waiter and he removed one of the menus.

"That was the wine carte, which we don't need. I asked him to bring some water. Is that okay?"

"That's perfect," he said. The menu was also written in English and he looked over some choices while Isabel did the same.

"Do you trust me?" she asked, setting down her menu.

Simon did the same and regarded her. "Yes, I trust you."

She obviously meant about what to order for dinner, but he trusted her with more than that.

She smiled. "I won't steer you wrong."

He knew that too.

They started dinner with prawns on a griddle with a light sauce of olive oil and garlic, followed by tender bits of octopus stewed in rice, and Simon found a kind of bravery he didn't know he had, as he tried new dishes sitting across from the girl he'd been dreaming of meeting in person for years.

He couldn't help the grin on his face any more than he could stop the bouncing heart in his chest, so full of a kind of joy he couldn't remember experiencing.

"I'm glad we didn't stay for the lecture at The Queen's English. This has been a lot more fun."

Isabel took a sip and set down her glass, a teasing look in her eyes. "That invitation you got for the poetry slam did seem like a lot of fun. Who was the girl?"

Was she just curious or did that interest carry a hint of something more?

"I didn't catch her name. She approached me right after you left and asked what had brought me there, and we got talking." He paused and purposefully met her eyes. "I was only making time until you came back."

Her cheeks colored and, after an intense, brief moment, she looked away from him.

Just then the waiter brought two thick slices of flan pudding for dessert.

"You're in for a treat," she said, picking up her spoon and ladling the sauce over her portion.

Simon did as she showed him.

She leaned closer and whispered, "It's almost as good as the pudding I make."

He winked at her. "I believe you."

After the meal, Simon called a taxi and they rode back to her neighborhood, sitting close to each other, her hand back in his, wishing the driver took the longest route to her building.

When they arrived, he insisted on seeing her to the door of her apartment. She unlocked the door and switched on the light in the foyer, then took a step inside, but he pulled back at her fingers.

"It's late, Isabel. I'm not coming in."

She slowed, and turned around to him, her fingers tangling with his. His thumb traced the skin above her wrist and she let out a low sigh. She stepped in his direction and Simon leaned toward her, the scent of caramel and sugar easily reaching him. If he kissed her, she'd taste of flan pudding.

Tell her. Tell her you're Elliot.

He leaned closer to her. "Can I kiss you, Isabel?"

The words flew out of his mouth.

Her eyes widened. "Simon—"

The elevator pinged and opened its doors. A young couple stepped out, wrapped up in each other, kissing even as they walked to the other apartment on the same floor. Simon stepped away from Isabel and cleared his throat, but the couple gave no indication of acknowledging anything or anyone around them. When the guy unlocked the door, the girl jumped and wrapped her legs around his waist. The kiss kept going as she pushed the door closed behind them.

"That's my neighbor," Isabel said in a low voice. "She's actually really nice. Just a little—" She grimaced. "That's her boyfriend."

Simon straightened. "Okay. I can see that."

Isabel nodded. "Well. . ."

"I—" He slipped his hands in his pockets. "I had a really good time today, Isabel. Thank you for showing me Lisbon." He'd lost the moment; it was too late for it now.

Isabel clasped her hands together. "You're welcome. I really enjoyed it too." She paused. "But maybe it's best we just—"

Just stay friends? Just pretend there was nothing between them? Just forget he asked to kiss her?

"Yeah," he added. "Maybe it is best." The time was not right yet.

Her voice softened. "We work together, Simon. And you'll be leaving soon."

"I know." Things were complicated enough already. "You don't have to explain."

They'd only be working together until Christmas break.

He could wait.

Chapter Fourteen

To: ameliefaithfulfriend@mail.com
From: elliotbestpenpal@mail.com

Dear Amélie,
It makes me sad that you think there are things you should delete when you write to me. I want you to talk to me about anything you want. I won't judge you. Write about your boss who doesn't take your suggestions, or the guy in the underground who didn't give up his seat (how dare he?). Write about the way your friend makes you crazy or how you wish you had an extra day on week-ends before going back to work on Monday. Especially tell me your dreams and your plans for the future. I want to hear all of them.

And this thing your friend wants you to do, that you want to do. I don't know what your fears are, but I'll tell you a little story. A while back I was faced with a similar decision. There was something that I wanted, but I was scared. What if it didn't work out? What if I put so much of my time and effort and so much of my heart into it and then nothing happened? Or worse, something happened but not what I wanted? I went a long time thinking about it, like you, staying awake at night and still not knowing what to do the next day.

And then one day I read two little words that helped me make a decision. What if? What if I didn't do anything about it? Was I prepared to live with the consequences of that, to always wonder what would have happened? What if I did it and it didn't turn out the way I wanted? At least I could say I tried, and I could live the rest of my days knowing I'd tried, with no regrets. Even if there was only one small chance, I had to take it.

What if, Amélie? What if you don't do it? Are you prepared to go through the rest of your life only dreaming about it? What if you try it? Even if others are better than you, they are not you. I want you to do something after you read this email. Get a sticky note and write down, I can do it, then stick it to the mirror in your foyer. Every morning before you leave, look at it and remember you have the strength to accomplish anything you want.

I'll be cheering you on, Amélie. I'll support you in whatever it is that makes you happy. You are not alone.

Well, that turned into an epistle. I better get my line in about the weather: it's definitely turning cooler. I can see Old Man Winter turning around the corner. I hope you're keeping warm.

Your friend always,
Elliot

P.S.—I don't think I'll be going back to London for Christmas. What are your plans?

༄

To: elliotbestpenpal@mail.com
From: ameliefaithfulfriend@mail.com

Dear Elliot,
Today I left work during lunch and didn't come back for two whole hours. I even turned off my phone and left my worries behind (and left good people in charge, so that eased my worries too).

The zoo is one of my favorite spots, and I have lots of good memories. When I was little, my grandmother and I went there often in the summer. She'd pack a lunch for us and we'd stay all day. First, we visited all the animals, then we had lunch in the shade, and talked about what we'd seen. On the way back, we'd stop at the formal gardens and I'd count all the roses until I ran out of numbers.

Have you ever noticed how memories are a two-edged sword? On one side, you're comforted by the happier times, and on the other side, it grieves your heart when you can no longer live those times again.

Such was a day like this, when I had to take time to myself and hang on the balance of the blade, torn between the happy memories and the bittersweet ones.

Your friend always,
Amélie

P.S.— Thank you for being my friend.

CHAPTER FIFTEEN

Isabel entered the teachers' lounge at the academy and Cristina waved at her from the corner. She took the chair next to her and set the lunch tray on the table.

"How crazy has it been today? I heard about the outbreak." Cristina pushed her plate to the side to make room.

Isabel took a sip from her glass of water. "It's been dubbed the Great Flu Outbreak. Ten students at home and counting. Three teachers who called in sick. I can't believe it's only Monday. If it keeps up, we might have to close earlier for the weekend."

Cristina leaned back. "That is not good. I'm making my kids wash their hands and use the hand sanitizer at all times." She took a bite. "What is Simon's take on this? I didn't see him at the meeting this morning."

"He sent a message saying he'd be a bit late this morning, but he didn't show up."

"That's odd. Did you try calling him?" Cristina stacked her knife and fork on the side of the plate.

Isabel wiped the corner of her mouth, buying some time before her answer. In truth, she'd been worried about him. It was out of character for Simon to be late and so cryptic about it. How appropriate was it for her to interfere? "I'll have the secretary ring him again."

Cristina raised her eyebrows. "The secretary? Why didn't you call him directly? You have his number, right?"

"Yes, I do." Isabel hesitated. She reached for a bread roll and broke off a piece. "It's complicated."

Cristina rested her elbows on the table and leaned in Isabel's direction. "Complicated? Did something happen between the two of you?"

Isabel took a forkful of peas and rice, and kept her eyes down. Had something happened? She was not sure what had passed between Simon and her. Was an almost-kiss worthy of being classified as eventful? Too much to think about. Isabel had tried not to analyze it.

Cristina pushed Isabel's plate out of reach. "Keeping your mouth full won't work. Spill it." She paused and smiled. "Well, swallow first and then tell me."

"There's not much to tell." Isabel set the fork down again. "We spent some time together. As friends," she hurried to add. "Nothing more."

Friends held hands, right? Friends had amazing dinners together and talked of everything; for sure they did.

"How much time and when? What did you do?"

Isabel held a hand up. "Calm down. Nothing exciting. On Friday I invited him over to cook dinner at the apartment. Don't look at me that way. He was going to eat frozen dinners."

Cristina shrugged. "Nothing wrong with frozen dinners. Lots of people buy them." The corner of her mouth quirked in a little smile. "But you wanted to save Simon from that kind of fate and had him over to cook dinner for him."

"He did the cooking and *I* supervised." She emphasized the word. "He bought the ingredients and he cooked them." He'd been a fast learner and Isabel had truly enjoyed teaching him some basic cooking. That's what friends did for each other.

"What else? That was on Friday. What happened on Saturday?"

"He asked me to go with him to this lecture at The Queen's English." She much rather preferred the bookstore when it was nearly empty on Sundays.

"Is that the English bookstore?" Cristina asked. "I'm sure you two could have found a better place to go out on a date."

"It wasn't a date. Just two friends going out together." If she kept repeating it, she might convince herself. "In any case, we didn't stay long."

Cristina touched her arm and her expression brightened. "That's good. You spent more time with Simon."

They had indeed spent more time together, but that only confused things between them a lot more. At least, on her part.

Isabel shrugged. "Yes, we did spend the rest of Saturday together. I took him sightseeing downtown and we ended up by the Praça do Comércio and the quay. We dined at this little restaurant on a side street, and then he took me home." The whole day had been perfect: the weather, the places, and especially the company. Until that moment at her apartment door.

Cristina's eyes brightened and she smiled wide. "Oooh, he kissed you at the door, didn't he?"

Isabel pulled Cristina's hand closer and shushed her. "Keep your voice down. Nothing happened."

Cristina scooted her chair closer to Isabel. "What do you mean nothing happened? You at least kissed, right? Tell me Simon Ackerley kissed you and he's the best kisser ever."

"I don't know if he is because we didn't kiss." Isabel paused over the memories of that moment by the apartment door. There had been no kissing, which was for the best, right? Then why did it feel like a missed opportunity?

"Oh," Cristina said, and her shoulders dropped. "I wanted to know if my theory is right."

"What theory?"

Cristina rested an elbow on the table and dropped her chin onto her hand. "Well, he's half American, but he was raised in England, so he must have the manners of a gentleman."

Isabel tried not to roll her eyes. "I want to see where this theory of yours is going."

Cristina waved her comment. "Bear with me. Since gentlemen don't spend the night with their girlfriends, and you know," she winked at Isabel.

Isabel rolled her eyes and shook her head. "Cristina, really."

"Well, it must be true, right? Code of conduct, honor and chivalry and all that." Cristina kept going, clearly enthused with her notion. "So I'm thinking these modern, sexually frustrated gentlemen must be great kissers." She smiled, as if proud of her logic. "Right?" she repeated. "How else are they going to show their manliness?" Cristina sighed. "But since you didn't let Simon kiss you, I can't prove I'm right."

Isabel squared her shoulders. "First, even if I had kissed him, I wouldn't have rated it or told you how—" she stuttered at the word "—manly he is. That's just preposterous. Second, how do you know it was me who stopped the kiss? We actually both agreed it might not be a good idea." The Academy's statutes only prohibited relationships while on campus, but they did work together on a daily basis. Things between she and Simon were awkward enough already without adding a personal relationship to the mix.

"Oh, pish-posh, Isabel. Kissing is always a good idea." Cristina stood and took her tray to the dishwashing cart, Isabel trailing behind her. "You need to let go and have fun. I'm telling you, Simon Ackerley is a great kisser. I can just tell." She puckered her lips, making a kissing sound. "That mouth of his. If I knew he wouldn't refuse me, I'd ask him for a kiss myself."

Isabel gaped, the tray in her hands. "Cristina," she said, unable to add anything more.

Cristina looked back on her way out and winked at Isabel. "Think about it."

Isabel didn't have to think about it. She'd been thinking about it all weekend; what it would be like to kiss him. And she thought about it some more during the next hour, while taking a tour of all the classes and updating her list of students who were out sick. She thought about nothing else but Simon and the almost-kiss.

They had both agreed to not complicate their relationship. They hadn't said it in so many words, but it had been clear. It was a mutual decision and he'd been fine with it, hadn't he?

So why hadn't he come to the book club on Sunday? She'd waited for him all morning, even staying over and enduring some not-so-scintillating discussions about the new book of the month, which she still hadn't read, therefore rendering her unable to participate. Friends endured boring literary clubs hoping their friends showed up, didn't they?

To make matters less tolerable, that girl who'd invited Simon to the poetry slam had been there at the bookstore as well, clearly looking for him. Did she not get the clue that he wasn't interested in her?

By the time Isabel had arrived home from the book club on Sunday, she'd almost convinced herself Simon had returned to England without saying goodbye.

Which wasn't true.

All of his things were still in his office, as she'd verified earlier.

He was only late this morning, even if it wasn't typical of him. Isabel had come to know him in the past few weeks, and he was always considerate and responsible, not to mention he had an impeccable work ethic.

Isabel returned to her office. Maybe something had happened and she should check on him. She reached for her phone and scrolled through the messages she'd sent earlier. He hadn't replied, and he hadn't even read the last ones. He'd been at home when he'd sent the last message, so she'd start there.

She accessed the staff files and looked up his address before turning off the computer. He lived not too far from the academy in an older neighborhood. Before she changed her mind about it, she exited the building and turned in the direction of Simon's apartment.

৩ৡৢ

The bell was ringing. Again. Shouldn't it at least wait fifty five minutes in between classes before going off? Had the academy changed the daily schedule without telling him?

Simon lifted his head from the pillow then slowly turned over until he faced the ceiling. Not at the academy. In his bed at the apartment. What was he still doing in bed? Was it morning again already?

The doorbell rang again, followed by a knock. So it wasn't his drug-induced and sickness-ridden imagination. Someone was at the door. Whoever it was, he or she could come back later. He wasn't ready to see anyone right now.

In between knocks and ringing, a familiar voice called out his name. "Come on, Simon. I know you're in there."

Isabel. As much as he wanted to see her, he was in deplorable conditions to do so.

Another knock followed a short pause. "I don't want to call the fire department to open the door."

No, he didn't want that either. Simon dragged himself to the edge of the bed and sat there for a minute, then gingerly stood, grabbing the blanket off the bed to wrap around himself. He then padded his way to the front door, one shuffle at a time.

Once in the foyer, he called out, "Hang on. I'm coming," and Isabel stopped knocking. He unlocked the door and released the latch then made his way to the nearest seat, in the living room.

"Simon?" Isabel came in and closed the door behind her.

"In here." With effort, he pulled himself into a sitting position. "How did you get inside the building?"

She sat across from him. "Your neighbor on the first floor came to the window to see what all the ringing was about. I told her I was your boss and you'd missed work today."

He smirked. "And she was only too happy to open the door for you."

Her mouth rose at the corners. "Something like that." She looked around the living room. "How long have you been like this?"

"Saturday night? Sunday morning, maybe?" It was all a bit muddled. "Did something happen at the academy?"

"Is that your roundabout way of asking me why I'm here?"

Simon shrugged. Typical Isabel. She didn't beat around the bush.

Isabel scooted to the edge of the sofa. "You didn't show up at the book club yesterday and you didn't come to work today."

"So you were worried about me?"

"No. I mean, yes." She looked toward the window and then back at him. "Maybe I was worried. Or maybe I just wanted to know why you were late."

Simon raised his head to look at her. "What time is it?" Had he really missed going to work this morning?"

"Just after lunch." She leaned forward. "Are you sick?"

Simon scrubbed his face and let out a long breath. "I'm so sorry I didn't show up. I didn't sleep very well, and I woke up late. Then I took some medicine…"

The medicine. What had he done with it?

"What kind of medicine did you take?" Isabel asked.

He gestured to the kitchen. "I got it at the service pharmacy yesterday. I think I left it on the counter."

Isabel stood and walked to the kitchen. She returned holding the small bottle. "What did you tell the pharmacist about your symptoms?"

Simon sat up to look at her. "Communication was a bit of a problem. Between his broken English and my very poor Portuguese, we got some words figured out." The translation app had helped with most of it.

"You do know this is a cold medicine with codeine?"

He shook his head and sighed loudly. "That would explain why it knocked me out so thoroughly." He'd taken a dose after returning from the pharmacy but in the morning, when he got out of bed, he was not feeling much better and had repeated the dose before sending a message to the school. That was the last thing he remembered. "I'm sorry I didn't come in, Isabel."

Isabel gave him a small smile. "You have a good excuse. And you're not the only one. Several teachers and students are out sick too. Whatever kind of virus it is, it's making its rounds at the academy."

"And you came to check on me?"

Her cheeks flushed. "We sent messages and tried calling you."

He hadn't heard any of them. "I'm not even sure where my phone is." He stood and padded to the bedroom. After poking around for a few minutes, he still didn't find it.

Isabel waited by the entrance to the kitchen when he returned.

"I don't know where I put it." He gave her a wide berth to keep the germs away from her and sat on a kitchen chair.

She drew her phone out of her coat pocket and within seconds a faint ringing came from somewhere in the living room. Simon moved to stand but she waved him off. He rested his chin on his hand and closed his eyes for a moment. His head felt fuzzy and the congestion hadn't cleared up any more than the day before. A cough scratched his throat and he stood to take a drink of water.

"I found it in your coat pocket," Isabel said, setting the phone down on the table. She watched as he drained the glass. "When was the last time you had anything to eat?" She removed her coat and draped it on the back of the opposite chair.

"I can't remember." He must have eaten something, but it was filed away in the vagueness of his memory. He sat back against the wall and clutched the blanket tighter around his shoulders.

Isabel approached the nearest cabinet. After a few moments of opening and closing doors and drawers, she stood in the middle of the kitchen with her hands on her hips. "You have nothing in your cupboards and the refrigerator is empty. What have you been living on, Simon Ackerley?"

He sat up a little. "What happened to the sugar and the flour?"

Isabel crossed her arms. "You're right. Excuse me. Almost nothing, except a kilo each of sugar, flour, and dry beans. Some butter and an expired Greek yogurt. It would take a miracle to cook anything with these ingredients, even for me."

Simon smiled weakly. "You're funny." He wanted to laugh, but his body hurt too much.

Isabel walked to him and pulled off the blanket. "Come on, let's go."

His hands jerked and he reached for the blanket but it was effectively too far. "I'd rather not go anywhere."

She pulled at his arm and tried to support him upright. "Just to the shower." Her fingers circled his bicep and he resisted the urge to flex his muscles.

"Do I smell that bad?" As if it weren't embarrassing enough for Isabel to see him sick.

"I'm not commenting on that, but it will make you feel better."

He winced. She didn't spare his feelings, did she?

At the door to his room, she hesitated. "Will you be able to do it by yourself?"

Simon sat on the bed and raised his eyes to her. "Are you going to help me?"

She eyed him with a raised eyebrow. "Are you trying to be fresh with me, Simon Ackerley?"

"I'm sorry. I don't know where that came from." He was definitely not feeling like himself. "Yes, I can shower by myself." Even if he had to sit down for it.

Isabel was right. The shower proved more therapeutic than he'd thought. He didn't shave and his body still hurt everywhere, but at least the fuzziness had dissipated some and he was clean and smelling much better. When he opened the bathroom door into the hallway, Isabel carried a small tray to the bedroom which she placed on the bedside table.

"Come on, let's put you back to bed until I get you something more substantial to eat." She pulled a pillow upright and turned down the sheets.

Simon sat down gingerly. "Did you change the bedding?"

"Of course. You don't put a freshly-showered sick person into the same linens."

When he reclined against the pillows, Isabel handed him a glass of water and two painkillers, which he promptly swallowed.

She had a cup of tea ready. "Lemon balm," she offered.

"Where did you get it?" He blew at the edge.

"Your neighbor on the first floor. She didn't mind sharing when I told her you were sick. It will make you feel better."

He was feeling a little better already. But it wasn't the tea or the shower, or even the fresh sheets.

It was Isabel's presence.

He must have dozed off after drinking most of the tea, and the medication had worked better than he'd thought. The blinds on the window were still up and the lights from the early evening outside blinked against the wall. Each day grew darker a little earlier as winter set in. Simon pushed the sheets back and a small smile crept to his lips. Isabel had come to see him because she was worried. That must be a good sign, right?

A knock sounded at the bedroom door and he sat up slowly.

Isabel peeked in. "How are you feeling?"

Simon passed a hand through his hair. "A little better, thank you. I thought you'd left by now."

She pushed the door open. "I did leave, but I came back. I have some broth for you. I'll bring it in, if you're ready."

He stood. "That's okay. I'll come to the kitchen."

By the time he sat at the small table, Isabel had placed a wide, shallow soup plate and some toast on the side with another cup of tea. He picked up the spoon. "Thank you, Isabel. I didn't expect you to come and cook for me."

She sat on the other chair. "It's just a simple rice broth. I didn't have the time to make chicken soup."

He took a spoonful. It was a cross between a vegetable soup and a thick broth, with well-cooked rice, onions, garlic, and carrots, all diced in small pieces. "This is very tasty." He was hungrier than he'd thought. "There's olive oil." He paused and savored the flavors again.

Isabel leaned on the table and rested her chin on her palm. "My grandmother used to make this for me when I was feeling poorly." Her eyes softened.

He could relate to that. Even though Mom had been gone for fifteen years, the smallest things sometimes prompted the hardest memories, the ones that took a toll on him.

He ate a second serving, surprising himself. Isabel saved the rest in the refrigerator and washed the few dishes while he sat watching her. He hadn't asked her and she'd come. Charlene, the girlfriend who'd lasted almost six months, had not even visited him at the hospital when he'd had an emergency appendectomy. Maybe comparing both women wasn't fair to either one of them, but a person's character proved truer in actions than words, didn't it?

Isabel removed the kitchen towel from her waist and hung it up on the small hook by the stove.

"Thank you," he said to her. "For everything." The words felt insufficient.

"You're welcome." Her cheeks pinked. "I'll bring you some soup tomorrow."

He probably had enough leftovers for two more meals but he wouldn't say no to a visit from her. "I'll be back to work on Wednesday."

"Don't rush it. If you're not feeling better, you can take the rest of the week off. We'd rather you're all recovered before coming back and getting yourself infected again, or infecting others."

He pulled the covers back around his shoulders and rose from the table.

"Please, don't get up on my account," she rushed to say. "I can see myself out."

"I can see you out. I'm feeling a little better."

She nodded, walking slowly, and Simon followed her to the front door. "Isabel, I'd like to apologize for what happened on Saturday night."

She shook her head. "Simon, it's okay. There's nothing to apologize for. We're both adults and smart enough to know that complicating things would not be good." She dropped her hands by her side and looked down for a moment. "It's okay," she repeated.

Had he read her wrong? He'd been so sure she was as interested in him as he was in her.

"I'm not sorry it happened," he said. "I'm just sorry it wasn't the right time."

"It's definitely not the right time for this conversation," she said. "You're still sick and need to go back to bed."

His shoulders dropped. "You're right. But I'd like to continue this conversation when I'm feeling better."

Isabel nodded. "I'll bring you some food tomorrow before I go to school," she repeated.

After she left, Simon returned to bed and picked up the mug with the tea, now cold, and took a drink of it. Being sick frustrated him, not only the physical weakness, but also the laying about doing nothing. There was work waiting for him at the academy.

And then there was Isabel, and the time he wanted to spend with her.

CHAPTER SIXTEEN

To: ameliefaithfulfriend@mail.com
From: elliotbestpenpal@mail.com

Dear Amélie,

I'm glad you take time for yourself. With the demanding job you have, it's good to find the quiet moments to slow down and think. I try to rest on Sundays and not think of work or the responsibilities that will be waiting for me on Monday mornings. After lunch, I spend time with family or friends, or doing something else worthwhile. Well, that sounds kind of conceited but I promise I'm just a regular guy trying to do the best he can.

There's someone I work with who reminds me of you. She's very dedicated to her job and works tirelessly. She helps others without thinking of herself and even though she holds a position of leadership, she always goes out of her way to make sure she treats *those around her fairly and justly, never expecting to be singled out.*

Sometimes I like to imagine that working with you would be similar.

You still haven't told me what you'll be doing for Christmas. Are you staying in or going away? Would you have the time for an old friend?

Your old friend,
Elliot

༄

To: elliotbestpenpal@mail.com
From: ameliefaithfulfriend@mail.com

Dear Elliot,
I'm very intrigued by this co-worker of yours. You obviously have great admiration for her. Do you see her outside of work?

I'm afraid I'm not as noble as she is. Yes, I am dedicated to my job and I try to treat people around me fairly, but that's as far as the similarities go. I rush to conclusions about too many things and I hold grudges for too long.

As for working with you, I can't even fathom the idea. We've been writing each other for so long, sometimes

I feel like I know you better than anyone else in my life. Such a crazy thought, isn't it?

I'm trying not to think about Christmas. I'll be by myself this year.

Always your friend,
Amélie

CHAPTER SEVENTEEN

*I*sabel looked at the clock on the kitchen wall. Simon should be arriving any time. She swiped her hands on the sides of her jeans, wishing the nerves would pass already. There was nothing to be nervous about, but the anticipation always got to her.

After spending a few days in bed, Simon had recovered and returned to the academy ready to work. He'd also been ready to have that conversation but she'd asked him for some time and he'd agreed to put it off for a little while.

At first, they had tiptoed around each other but, after a couple of awkward days, they decided not to spend time together on Friday evenings and Saturdays, as much as she would have liked to.

During the weekdays at the academy, Isabel made a conscious effort to treat Simon professionally and she'd begun to appreciate his presence and all he did to improve the conditions there. He was an invaluable asset and the changes he'd made would benefit the academy for years to come.

But Sundays were different. Sundays were a day of truce. As careful as they were to keep their distance from each other at work, cooking together after book club had become her favorite thing to do, and she couldn't even explain to herself how much she looked forward to it. No mention of work, no thinking of the almost-kiss—just two friends spending time together.

The door bell rang and Isabel startled. She rushed to open it and found Simon holding several grocery bags in his hands.

"What's all this?" She took a couple of bags and let him through, then closed the door.

"All the ingredients to make an authentic New England clam chowder," he replied, already emptying the groceries onto the kitchen counter.

She joined him, and they quickly sorted the fresh ingredients into kinds. "I like what I see, but I have two questions."

"Go ahead." Simon opened the door to the pantry and took his apron, the one he always wore when they cooked together, black with a border of red hearts.

"First, where's New England? And second, what's a chowder?"

"New England is a geographic region in the northeastern United States, comprised of Maine, Vermont, New Hampshire, Massachusetts, Rhode Island and

Connecticut. I told you my mother was from Boston, where my parents met." He took the vegetables to the sink and started rinsing them.

Something wonderful curled in Isabel's chest as she watched the way he moved so comfortably in her kitchen, in her house, knowing where everything was and doing things the way she liked.

She paused to appreciate the moment but he continued, oblivious to her thoughts. "A chowder is a rich soup with potatoes and seafood, but there are lots of variations. The clam chowder is the most famous in that part of the country."

"And you know how to cook this? I'm impressed. Sounds like you've been paying attention to the cooking lessons."

Simon chuckled. "Not quite."

She raised an eyebrow at his honesty.

"Well, I mean—I have been paying attention, but I don't want to mess it up. Here, let me show you." He pulled out his phone, tapped the screen a few times, and held it up for her. "I have a recipe and I'm hoping we can do it together."

She took the phone from him and scanned through the recipe. "It's almost like a stew. Not hard at all. I'm sure you could make it without my help, but I'm excited to cook this." She returned the phone. "Why don't you start chopping the vegetables while I clean the clams?"

"Your chopping skills are better than mine," he said matter-of-factly.

Isabel dropped the clams into a large bowl and covered them with water. "You chop just fine," she said.

They stood side by side working at the sink and when she turned her face up to meet his eyes, she found his already on her, warm and expectant, belied by a hint of intensity.

"What?" she asked, hoping to distract him from the seriousness in his expression.

He opened his mouth as if to say something, but then shook his head and smiled. "I'm just glad to be doing this with you. That's all."

That was plenty. She was glad too, more than she ever thought she would. "Are you faffing about, Simon Ackerley?" she teased. If she acknowledge his words, the conversation would likely go in a different direction, one she was still not ready for.

He reached for celery. "No, chef."

"Let's get to work then. I'm hungry."

After carefully washing the clams, she placed them in a large pot. "What if I stew them in some white wine?" she asked. She opened the cabinet where she usually kept the cooking wine, but found the spot empty.

Simon paused. "I didn't buy any, sorry. You said you didn't drink."

"I did say that, didn't I? When Cristina came over with her boyfriend."

He nodded. "I didn't even think of cooking wine."

Isabel turned on the gas burner for the clams and reached for the bacon. "It's totally fine, don't worry about it. I can follow the recipe for once," she said easily.

"Not following a recipe. Is that a Portuguese thing or an Isabel thing?" Simon placed the chopped onions and celery in different containers.

"It's not so much that I can't follow the instructions, because I can." She stirred the bacon pieces so they wouldn't stick to the pan. "I always feel like I need to add my own flavor, not to show off but to make it more like a piece of me." She shrugged. "It sounds kind of dumb when I say it like this."

"No, no, it doesn't. I understand what you mean. I think most people are not confident enough in their cooking skills to deviate much from a recipe. I know I'm not," he added. "I'm glad you're teaching me to be more adventurous."

"I think you're doing great," Isabel said with a smile. "The first time you came you didn't even know the difference between a paring knife and a chopping knife."

They spent the next hour finishing the clam chowder, easy conversation flowing between them. When they were done, Isabel ladled the soup into bowls and Simon added the garnishes of crispy bacon bits and finely chopped celery leaves. With the potatoes and clams in the rich broth, it looked very appetizing.

She took a spoonful, blew on it before eating, and slowly let the flavors meld in her mouth. "This is so good," she said in between more careful bites.

Simon nodded, busy with blowing on his spoon and eating his own hot chowder. After swallowing, he said, "It's been a while since I had a bowl of this, but it tastes just like the one my mom used to cook."

"Food has a way of bringing people together to make happy memories, doesn't it?" Isabel said, thinking about all the times she'd spent in the kitchen with Avó Marta.

"Just like we're doing right now," Simon said.

His tone was comfortable, with the kind of contentment that came from familiarity with someone close. He set down his spoon and reached for her left hand, holding it for a moment, almost as a caress.

Her breath stilled and goose bumps raised on her skin, even as he let go of her fingers.

He resumed eating his chowder, not even realizing how his small touch had left such a large impression on her.

How was she supposed to go about the rest of the day with him and pretend it didn't affect her?

༄

Only a few more days and school would be out for Christmas holiday. Isabel turned on the desktop computer and adjusted the security card around her neck. The grades for first term were due on Friday, and she had to check the reports from all the teachers. Even though the academy had an online portal, Isabel also sent letters home, since most parents still preferred to have printed reports.

She pulled out her cell phone and scrolled through the messages. A small smile grew on her lips. Simon had sent a text to her in the early morning.

Thank you for the fabulous dinner last night.

He'd come by again after book club and they'd cooked as they did on Sundays, laughing and talking about everything. No worries, no agendas, just the best of times she'd had in a long while.

She typed a message back. **You cooked most of it.**

But you supervised, came his reply.

Just admit it already, you don't need supervision.

Maybe not, but I cook better with you.

She did too. Everything turned out better in his company.

After a few minutes without a reply, she returned to the online portal and the student reports.

When her phone pinged with a message, Isabel reached for it eagerly, hoping it was Simon again, and berating herself for the expectation.

Why did she always put herself through this during the weekdays? She'd been the one to say no to Fridays and Saturdays and yet, here she was, counting down until the following Sunday when they'd spend time together again. As if she wouldn't see him every day at the academy.

Miss Antunes, please come to my office.

It was from Dr. Varela, not Simon. She checked the time. The staff meeting would start in twenty minutes. Couldn't he wait until then?

When she entered the office, Simon was there. She smiled at him but he only looked at her with barely a nod.

Dr. Varela stood. "Thanks for coming, Miss Antunes." He gestured toward one of the chairs. "Please, take a seat."

Isabel sat on the closest chair and Simon took the other. She tried to catch his eye, but he turned ahead and didn't look at her. Her confidence wavered. What was going on? She clutched her hands on her lap.

"Miss Antunes, something serious has come to my attention," Dr. Varela said. He sat and leaned forward. "But before I tell you what has happened, I need you to tell me if you know where your security card is."

"Yes, of course I know." Isabel pulled the lanyard from around her neck and placed the card on the desk.

Dr. Varela reached for it and turned it in his hand, examining first one side and then the other before checking the key attached to the back. He set the card on top of the desk in front of him, and out of Isabel's reach.

"What's going on?" she asked.

"I'm afraid there's been some misappropriation of funds." He paused to look straight at her. "It's not the first time either."

Isabel clutched her hands. "How did it happen?"

"We first noticed a small inconsistency in May. It was insignificant and we probably wouldn't have given it any more thought, but then it happened again in June, on the last week of classes." Dr. Varela leaned forward on his desk. "Once every day until the last day."

Isabel sat straight in her chair and grabbed the sides as a weight dropped in her stomach with the feeling of a sinking stone. "Go on."

Dr. Varela cleared his throat. "At first, we couldn't trace the origin of these inconsistencies. Then they stopped during the summer. But with classes back in session in September, the behavior resumed. That's when we hired Mr. Ackerley to look into it." He gestured at Simon.

Her hands turned cold on her lap. "Why was I not told any of this?"

Dr. Varela's neck reddened and Simon rested his elbows on his knees without saying a word. Isabel glanced at Simon, still trying to understand what was happening.

"You had just lost your grandmother, Miss Antunes," said Dr. Varela. "You were gone for a few days and I didn't want to bother you."

"It's my job to be bothered." She reined in her voice. "Whatever the problem is. You know that."

Dr. Varela coughed dryly into his fist.

All this time, they'd never mentioned anything to her. Simon had never told her. "How often did it happen?" she asked.

"As little as once a week and as much as two or three times. There isn't a clear pattern. Sometimes there's a break in between weeks."

This couldn't be happening. She took a breath, guessing—knowing—what was coming next. "But you've been able to trace it now."

Dr. Varela picked up her security card. "Unfortunately, it's been traced to this card."

Her shoulders dropped. Dr. Varela was not even going to ask her if she'd done it. "Am I fired?"

Simon finally had a reaction. He straightened and shook his head. "Isabel—"

Dr. Varela held a hand up. "Did you do it, Miss Antunes?"

She stood and the men stood as well. "Does it matter if I say no? If I say I didn't do it?"

"Of course it matters." Simon stepped towards her and she retreated.

Dr. Varela came around his desk. "Have you left your card and key unattended at any time?"

She shook her head. "No, I follow protocol. I wear it around my neck when at the academy and I take it home with me at the end of each day. I need it with me to pass security anyways." She dropped her hands. "You know that." Everybody at the academy knew that. She always had the card and key on her, didn't she? "So, what now?" she asked.

"We haven't called the police—" Dr. Varela started.

"We're not at that point yet." Simon turned to Dr. Varela. "We need more time before we contact the local authorities."

Isabel touched the side of her forehead, where a dull pain threatened to blow into a full-fledged headache. Her hands were cold and clammy and she absently noted the tightness in her chest.

Dr. Varela returned to his seat. "As I was saying, the police won't be involved yet, but we'd like you go on Christmas holiday earlier." He coughed again. "Just don't leave the city, please."

She was the main suspect, of course. Her card had been used without her knowledge or consent, but not once had Dr. Varela said they knew someone else had done it. Isabel grabbed the back of the chair. "What about the term grades? And mailing out the reports?"

"The secretaries will take care of that," Dr. Varela said.

Isabel turned to look at Simon for a moment. He was flushed, his hair mussed, and he didn't even wear a necktie. She'd never seen him without one at the academy.

Simon grabbed her elbow. "Isabel, we'll get to the bottom of this."

Isabel stepped away from him. "Will you need my computer password, Mr. Ackerley?" she asked him.

"Yes, please. We'll add it to the list of passwords," Dr. Varela said. "I'll call you later, Miss Antunes. We'll have some questions for you."

She nodded curtly. "Of course." She walked out with her shoulders straight and her chin up.

Simon closed the door, arguing with Dr. Varela in low tones.

When Isabel entered her office, she looked around for a moment. Her shoulders ached from the tension in her neck and she unclenched her fists. She walked to her desk and turned off the computer, then reached for the tablet in the drawer and set it on the desk.

Simon flung the door open, holding on to the door knob. "What are you doing?"

"What does it look like I'm doing?" She opened the bottom drawer and retrieved her purse. "I'm going home." She walked around the desk. "Excuse me."

"Isabel, wait." Simon touched her upper arm. "I know you didn't do this."

"But you knew they suspected me and you never said anything." Her shoulders slumped and her voice softened. "Why didn't you tell me, Simon?"

He shook his head and blew out a breath. "I thought I'd have the proof to exonerate you by now."

But he didn't have any evidence and he couldn't help her.

She reached in her purse and handed him the keys to the academy. "Please give these back to Dr. Varela."

Simon followed her to the courtyard. "I'll come see you after school."

"Don't, Mr. Ackerley."

"Isabel, please—"

"I think I should probably find a lawyer." Maybe she could call Jacinta. Her cousin might have some contacts or know of someone who could recommend a lawyer.

She kept walking. If she stopped now, her legs would buckle.

༄༅

Simon returned to Dr. Varela's office and entered without knocking. "I asked you to wait to tell her. I only need a few more days to solve this."

Dr. Varela looked up from his desk and resumed stacking papers. "The academy board wants to be done with this matter by the time classes start in January."

"I'm telling you, I don't need that long. Isabel Antunes has not done this." He ground out the words and clenched his hands. How could they all jump to conclusions so fast? "Just because it's her card accessing the system doesn't mean she's the one doing it."

"Mr. Ackerley, calm down, please." Dr. Varela pointed to a chair.

Simon dropped into it and held himself back from scrubbing a hand over his face. "Are you really calling the police?"

Dr. Varela let out a long breath. "It's complicated. We're not a public school, but this is a criminal activity. We just need to tie the card to the user. It will be easier if we present a clean case when the authorities have to be called in." He crossed his arms. "Are you sure it's not Miss Antunes?"

Simon sat up. "I am positive. I just can't prove it yet. Whoever is behind this knows exactly what he's doing and Miss Antunes does not have the kind of digital background to pull this off. But I have set up a trap and next time they use her card number to make a transfer, I will have the necessary information to trail it back to its source." It was only a question of time. "What did you do with Miss Antunes' card?"

Dr. Varela stood and came around his desk. "I locked it away in the academy's vault along with her key."

Simon rose from the chair and walked to the door. "That's perfect. I'll be able to figure out how the culprit is doing this the next time the card is used." And with the card locked away, Isabel would have the alibi to prove she was not involved.

He swung the door open and Dr. Varela stopped him. "Mr. Ackerley, please remember that as far as anyone knows, you're Miss Antunes' assistant. You must go on with her duties in her absence."

At lunch time, Simon dialed Isabel's number. When she didn't answer, he sent her a message. **I'm coming to see you.**

Her reply came within a few minutes. **I'm not home.** Not home? Had she left the city?

The phone pinged with another message from her. **Don't worry. I'm still in town. If the police call for me, I'll turn myself in.**

Isabel, that's not funny. I'll be able to prove your innocence this week.

He waited for a reply from her, but it didn't come.

The rest of the school day dragged by, everyone demanding his attention with problems he didn't want to deal with. It should be Isabel at the academy, not him. Apparently, Dr. Varela had told the faculty and students that Isabel was taking some time off due to sickness. She wouldn't like the lie and neither did Simon. But coming out with the real reason might spook the person behind the money transfers and that would place everything he'd been working for in danger of collapsing.

By the time Simon arrived at his apartment, his mood had not improved. He set up the laptop on the kitchen table and opened the academy's online portal. The last activity had pushed at the limits of the daily transfers. A few more euros over and it would flag the authorities for sure.

But it was getting close now. He only needed one more transfer and the online tracker would attach itself to the transaction and tell him everything he needed to know. Just a matter of time.

Before going to bed, Simon sent Isabel another text. **Are you home?**

Her reply came immediately. **Please don't come.**

I'm not. Just wanted to tell you I'm thinking about you. It was more than thinking, wasn't it? He couldn't get her out of his mind. **Tell me what you need I'll be there.**

Thanks, Simon.

When can I see you?

There was a pause before she replied, **I don't know.**

Simon placed the phone on the bedside table and sat on the edge of the bed.

He couldn't think of what to say to her. Isabel was alone, accused of something she hadn't done, and wondering why he hadn't said anything to her, probably doubting his friendship.

The only thing he could do was concentrate on the work and catch the digital signature of the person responsible, and clear her name as soon as possible.

That was all he could do for now. Even if she didn't want to see him.

CHAPTER EIGHTEEN

To: elliotbestpenpal@mail.com
From: ameliefaithfulfriend@mail.com

Dear Elliot,
I'm devastated. I've been wrongly accused of something too serious to even fathom. And a person whom I trusted knew I was being investigated and never said anything to me. It makes me sad.

My hands are trembling too much and I'm too cold.

I don't know what's going to happen.

Please think of me and send me any good vibes you can spare,

Amélie

∽⚬∾

To: ameliefaithfulfriend@mail.com
From: elliotbestpenpal@mail.com

Dear Amélie,
Please, please, please have courage and stay strong. Everything will be all right.

My thoughts are with you.

Always,
Elliot

P.S.—You won't be alone for Christmas.

CHAPTER NINETEEN

*T*he sound of the rain hitting the exterior blinds woke her. Isabel slid out of bed and pulled at the cord to bring the blinds up. It was hard rain, running down the glass and onto the marble sill, and out against the side of the building. She put a hand to the pane and the skin on her arms turned into gooseflesh. The neighbor across the street had forgotten to pull in the unmentionables drying on the line from the night before. Too late to save them now.

She wrapped herself in a fleece robe and reached for her cell phone. The display read after eight o'clock. After the night she'd had, it wouldn't have surprised her to have slept the morning away. It had been well after two in the morning by the time she'd succumbed to the physical and emotional exhaustion of Monday's events.

In the space of half a day, she'd gone through almost all the phases of grief and loss. The loss of her naïveté in assuming everything was well. The grief of finding out someone doubted her integrity. Eight years at the academy dedicating all her time and skills and now her reputation was ruined. Even if she could prove she was not the one embezzling the funds, how would she professionally recover from this? Word would get out, one way or another. People would always doubt her, always wonder if she'd done it. Her career in school administration was ruined.

She'd taken the long way home in disbelief over the accusation, going through all the scenarios of how someone could have gotten hold of her security card. Once inside her apartment, only the memories of Avó Marta had stopped her from crashing a stack of plates against the tiled floor. The plates didn't deserve it, and no one else was around to clean the mess for her. But the anger of knowing someone at the academy had been using her card to misappropriate funds was almost too much to deal with.

The tears came after that, fast and furious at first, then spent and sporadic, leaving her empty and tired and with a boulder-sized headache. Crying never solved anything, but it was inevitable at times.

And then Elliot's words had made their way to her, his words about courage and staying strong. How she wished she could talk to him, pick up a phone and tell him everything, hear him say the words she'd only ever seen written. What did he sound like? How deep was his English accent?

After Simon's text, Isabel had slept fitfully but when she woke in the morning to the sound of battering rain, she knew what to do. Not even a hint of a doubt marred her decision.

Her phone rang from the living room and she stood to find it. It was her cousin. She'd sent her a quick text asking if she knew of someone in Lisbon who could refer a trustworthy civil lawyer. Jacinta had Romano cousins all over the country and maybe they could tell Isabel who to contact.

"Jacinta, good morning. Thanks for calling me back."

"Of course, Isabel. My cousin Filipe knows lots of people in Lisbon and he gave me the name and number of a good lawyer."

Isabel wrote down the information. "This is really helpful, thank you."

"Are you in trouble?" Jacinta asked.

Isabel paused and took a breath. "Maybe. I don't know yet." She briefly told Jacinta of the accusations against her.

"That's crazy," Jacinta said.

"I know. It came as a shock, as you can imagine. The man hired by the academy to find out who the identity of the embezzler is trying to prove I didn't do it, and he's hopeful he can get the evidence before the director calls the police."

"Can you trust this guy? If he's working for the academy, he might not have your best interests in mind."

"If I can't trust him, I'm in big trouble." Isabel hesitated then added, "It's Simon."

"Simon? Isn't he the guy who went over to your apartment to cook with you? He's the same man they hired?"

Isabel sighed. "The very same one. Simon Ackerley."

"Oh boy," Jacinta said.

"I know. It's complicated."

"I'd say."

Isabel glanced at the time on the old-fashioned alarm clock. "I'm sorry to cut this short, but I'm running late," Isabel said. "Thanks for the referral. I'm hoping I won't need it, but it's good to have."

"I'm hoping you won't either. Keep me posted."

After hanging up with Jacinta, Isabel finished getting ready and called a taxi to pick her up. She had one hour to get to the other side of Lisbon and couldn't be late.

Even though she couldn't control some of what was going on in her life at the moment, she could control how she reacted to it.

Big changes were coming.

෧෨෨

Isabel glanced at the clock display on the microwave. She was expecting Cristina to arrive at any moment. After the long day Isabel had, she'd sent a message to her friend to join her for dinner, if she didn't mind coming out at night in the bad weather.

When the doorbell rang, Isabel set the wooden spoon on the plate and ran to open the front door.

Cristina rushed in and threw an arm around Isabel's shoulders. "Isabel. How are you?"

Isabel hung Cristina's coat on the hook and placed the wet umbrella in the stand. "I can't believe you came out to see me in this weather."

Cristina followed Isabel to the kitchen. "Are you kidding me? The zombie apocalypse wouldn't keep me away." She sat on the tall stool by the counter. "Simon Ackerley is walking around like his best friend died and Dr. Varela has left the academy in Simon's hands. And Simon is not saying anything to anyone so I had to come and see you."

Isabel stirred the pot. "I'm okay, Cristina. And the academy is in good hands with Simon." She truly believed it. Amazing how her change of attitude had also shifted her perception of Simon's role at the academy. "He has been following me for over three months. He knows what to do."

Cristina crossed her leg and leaned forward. "Are you sick, like Dr. Varela said?"

"No, I'm not." Isabel turned off the gas burner.

"Then why are you not at the academy?"

Isabel reached for two soup plates from the cupboard. "I'm taking some time off." She set the plates down across from Cristina. "I registered for the cook-off competition."

Cristina jumped from the stool and screamed. "What?!" She came around the counter and grabbed

Isabel's hands. "You did? You entered the competition? When?"

Isabel smiled. "Today. At the Tivoli Resort. They had open applications and I went." She filled the soup plates with the caldo verde soup and retrieved two spoons from the drawer. "Watch it. It's hot."

They sat at the kitchen table. Cristina hadn't stopped smiling, her eyes wide and proud. "What did they have you do? Were there many others there?"

"I think the heavy rain put off a lot of people. The organizers said they'd been expecting more applications." Isabel blew at the soup and stirred it. "I first waited in line for almost one hour. Then I filled in an application and they told everyone there to come an hour after that. I walked back to the hotel's lobby and sat there. When I came back, they interviewed most applicants present, which meant waiting around a little more."

"What about the cooking? There was no cooking involved?" Cristina took a spoonful of her soup.

"Not today. After the interview they said to expect a call if I was selected for the cooking audition."

Cristina touched her forehead. "I don't know how you can be so calm about this. If I were the one waiting for the phone call, I'd be a wreck. Did they tell you when they're calling?"

Isabel set the spoon down. "I got the call an hour ago." She rested her chin on her hand and smiled.

Cristina clasped her hands. "You did? You're going on the cooking auditions? My gosh, Isabel. You knew from the beginning and you didn't say?"

Isabel chuckled lightly. "You were the one with all the questions."

Cristina scraped the spoon against the bottom of the soup plate and finished her last bite. "So how does it all work? Did they say?"

"Tomorrow they'll put all fifty applicants at different stations and we'll be cooking in front of three judges. There will be a secret ingredient and I have to come up with something original."

"Like on the Food Channel," Cristina said.

Isabel nodded. "Yes, it's similar. The top twenty applicants who pass will then be chosen for the TV show. And the show works like this—" She paused and ticked her fingers. "On day one, the first round is taped in front of a live audience. The contestants receive a basket of ingredients and they have to make a three-course meal in front of a panel of judges. On day two, the contestants get a day off to plan their menus while the taped show goes on national TV, and people can vote online or through text message for their favorites. On day three, the four contestants with higher votes go face to face on a show broadcast live and are judged by four professionals."

Cristina blew a breath. "Wow. I can't even fathom. What are you doing to prepare for all this?"

Isabel shrugged. "Nothing. There's nothing I can do to prepare. I don't know what the secret ingredients will be tomorrow. I'll have to improvise and hope I can remember all the things Avó Marta taught me."

"You'll be great, Isabel. I know it." Cristina stood and placed their plates in the sink. "And look at you, all calm and confident."

"Surprisingly, I am calm." She hadn't been in the beginning; far from it. "I'm sure everything will be all right." Not only the competition, but also the matter at the academy. There was only so much she could do and worrying about what was out of her hands didn't help at all.

Isabel stood and walked to the sink. "Okay, there's more to it. If I pass the cooking audition, I'll come home to pack a light suitcase and I'll let you know. When I return to the resort, they'll put me in a hotel room and I can't contact anyone, or have a phone, watch TV, be on the internet or anything. I'll have to sign a confidentiality agreement."

"That's insane. For how long?"

"Until I'm kicked out or until the end of the live show. I do get to add someone's name to the list of guests coming to the live broadcast, and I'll put your name on it. They'll call you and ask if you want to come in to the event if I make it that far."

Cristina flicked Isabel's arm. "You bet I'll be there. I wouldn't miss it for anything."

Isabel wiped her hands dry. "You just have to promise me you won't tell Simon. He's got a lot going on right now and I don't want him to worry."

"There's something going on at the academy, isn't there?"

"I'm sorry I can't tell you. I don't even know

everything that's happening there." Simon was working on it and somehow she believed he'd figure it out. "Hopefully, it will all be solved soon."

After Cristina left, Isabel put the leftovers in the refrigerator and washed the few dishes in the sink. She settled in bed with her favorite blanket and the new book she'd bought last week, but her mind was elsewhere.

Isabel had contacted Dr. Varela and explained she'd be involved in a project for a few days and might be out of reach. She gave him the competition publicist's email address if he needed to get word of anything to her. And she'd assured him she'd be in Lisbon the whole time. Technically, it was Almada, on the bank across the river, but it was still part of the Greater Lisbon Area.

Her only regret was Elliot. She didn't have the time to tell him all that was going on and she'd be unable to reply to his next email right away. But she planned to tell him about the cooking competition when it was all over. Maybe it was time to even tell him everything else. His last email had hinted he wanted to come to Lisbon for Christmas. Or had she misread it?

In the past few months, their correspondence had taken on a more intimate tone. They'd started sharing more details about what mattered to each one, asking questions and trying to guess what kind of jobs they had or what they thought about certain subjects. They'd even discussed past relationships.

Sometimes Isabel told herself it was just Elliot being polite and expressing a friendly interest. But other times she let herself think it was something more. It was Elliot wanting to know who she really was, what she did, and what she thought of him. She wanted the same thing. She wanted to know the real Elliot, the man behind the letters, the friend who knew so much about her, and yet not enough.

The old fear was still there, the one which had been holding her back from asking more of him, a fear Elliot probably shared. What if they met in person and he didn't like her? Or she didn't like him? Was she prepared to take the risk of losing her best friend? How would she go on without his letters?

And then there was Simon, who'd turned out to be the friend she never planned for. She'd never seen it coming, this friendship with him. What would he say when she told him she'd been corresponding with a guy for more than half her life? A guy who held such a special place in her heart. Did it even matter what Simon thought of Elliot? As much as she wanted to say it didn't, more and more Simon's opinion was important to her and the attachment between them was undeniable.

Isabel closed her eyes and took a steadying breath. The conflict within her was much too real. How did she even find herself in this confusing situation with such strong feelings for two different men?

One thing she knew: it was time. If Elliot wanted to come to Lisbon and meet her, she'd say yes.

CHAPTER TWENTY

To: elliotbestpenpal@mail.com
From: ameliefaithfulfriend@mail.com

Dear Elliot,
I'll be away from a computer and cell phone for a few days. I'll tell you everything when I return.

Always,
Amélie

Chapter Twenty-one

*O*n Thursday morning very early, Simon woke up cold in his bed. The rain beat hard against the windows and he wiped the frost from the pane with the tip of his fingers. Half the city hid behind a curtain of fog, hanging low by the river and muting the colors of the buildings and the occasional red tiled roof peeking through. Lisbon was a wet, gray city, not so much unlike London on a day like this.

He pulled a blanket from the bed and wrapped it around his shoulders. He hadn't quite gotten used to the lack of central heating in the apartment and he'd left the space heater in the living room. Maybe he should get another heater to use in the bedroom.

It was the last day of classes before the Christmas holiday with class parties in the morning and an academy-wide assembly after lunch. Afterward, the upper classes ran a Santa workshop for the lower grade classes, which was always very popular, from what he'd heard. The marks for the first term would be posted tomorrow, the letters to the parents had been mailed, and the last updates on the online portal had gone up glitch-free.

If he could just get the digital trail to pan out, he'd clear the suspicion from Isabel and turn in the information about the criminal to Dr. Varela, who'd hopefully call the authorities on the real culprit.

Once he had everything behind him, he could meet Amélie for Christmas, if she'd have him.

Simon walked to the small kitchen table where he'd left his laptop the night before. He filled the kettle with water, put it on the stove, and grabbed a teabag of morning blend Earl Grey from the cupboard. He'd have to buy some of that lemon-balm herbal tea Isabel had made when he was sick. The taste had grown on him.

While he waited for the water to boil, he ran a finger across the touchpad. The screen came to life. He clicked on the small window with the tracker software and red trails filled the gaps.

Simon stilled, his eyes wide and fingers hovering over the small area below the keyboard. This was it, what he'd been waiting for weeks. A transaction had occurred in the early morning, and even though the perpetrator had used Isabel's card number to access the site and make the transfer, the card signature was different. Someone had made a copy of Isabel's security card. Now he just had to find out who.

With a few clicks, he made a copy of the trail and recorded the ISP address. Then he made duplicates of the information and burned them to a flash drive, making three copies of that.

Simon couldn't wipe the smile off his face while he sent a quick message to Dr. Varela, finished drinking his cup of tea, and got dressed for the day. When he stepped outside, the temperature was colder than in the days before, the rain fell in sheets, and his umbrella had a bent spoke at an odd angle. He adjusted the lapels of his overcoat and grinned again.

It was a glorious day.

∞

Simon stood in the center of the academy's atrium as the students left.

"Merry Christmas, Mr. Ackerley," a first grade girl said as she hugged him around the legs. He'd gotten used to the gesture from the younger children in the past few weeks.

He placed a hand on her head. "Merry Christmas, Carla. Have a good holiday."

The day was almost done now. Who knew that such a busy day could go by so slowly? Dr. Varela was meeting with Simon after the students left, and Simon was anxious to share his findings.

He returned to his office and grabbed the laptop. Across the hallway, in front of Isabel's closed office door, sat a pile of brightly colored presents and homemade cards. Children had come throughout the day and had left them for their beloved director. They missed her.

He missed her, more than he thought possible in just three days. The last email he'd received from Amélie concerned him, but he couldn't confront Isabel with something she hadn't told him. Cristina knew something. She'd been avoiding him all week, and she'd never done that before. As soon as he met with Dr. Varela, he'd go and talk to her.

Dr. Varela crossed the atrium and Simon followed. The older man closed the door behind them after they entered his office.

"Have a seat, Mr. Ackerley. What have you been able to find out?"

Simon opened his laptop and navigated to the window with the electronic trail. "There was a transaction early this morning. I was able to pin the tracker onto the user."

"What does that mean?" Dr. Varela asked.

"Imagine someone coming into your office at night. You know they're coming so you've left sticky black paint all over the floor, which they miss since they're sneaking in and keeping the lights off." He pointed at the screen. "It's the same here, except electronically. I knew they were using Miss Antunes' card number from the last tracking I did, so I left a trap for that purpose and I caught them sneaking in."

Dr. Varela looked up from the screen. "But how

is that possible? I told you I locked her card in the academy's vault."

Simon's lips rose in a smile. "And that was the best thing to do, because it proved my suspicion that she was not the one using it for diverting the funds."

"How did they do it then?" Dr. Varela's expression furrowed.

"It was a clever move from the person behind this. I still haven't figured out how he had the opportunity, but at some point he was able to make a 3D copy of Miss Antunes' key. Then he used another academy card and transposed the magnetic strip to a copy of her card." Simon hoped to find out if Isabel remembered leaving her card and key behind or unattended. She'd never even noticed it missing.

"A 3D copy?"

"Dr. Varela, do you know what the science lab has under the white cover sitting on the back counter?"

"The big box on the west wall?"

Simon nodded. "You didn't even know that your academy owns a 3D printer, did you? A really nice model too." As the fifth and sixth grade pranksters had proved.

Dr. Varela raised his eyebrows. "And a copy of the counterfeit card and key were enough?"

"The person behind this operation is savvy and probably has done this before," Simon added. "He knew how to duplicate the information from Miss Antunes' card onto the copy. That's how I also knew that she couldn't be involved. It's not her area of expertise. I'm recommending new security cards and keys, by the way." His full assessment report included more detailed recommendations.

"I agree," said Dr. Varela. "Now tell me you know who did this."

Simon handed him the flash drives with the information. "I have a copy of the tracker and the ISP address. When you call the authorities, they'll be able to find out the identity of this person." He paused. "I can tell you who I think it is, and I'll be very surprised if I'm wrong about it."

Dr. Varela leaned back in his chair. "Well, who is it?"

Simon held back a smile. "Dr. Varela, who has unchecked access to all the rooms on campus?" He didn't wait for Dr. Varela's reply. "You do, of course, and Miss Antunes. I've been given that responsibility and I'm sure the security company does too. And then the janitors do."

Dr. Varela frowned. "The janitors?"

"Think about it. It's the perfect cover. They have access to all the rooms on campus, nobody ever questions what they do, and they can come and go at any time." Simon turned to the laptop and navigated to the staff files. "I checked the employee records. Manuel Silva has been working at the academy since its opening. I confirmed he doesn't speak English. But Carlos Macedo served in the army. I wouldn't be surprised if his specialty was in electronics. He's been working for three years at the academy and he lied about not speaking English, although he hides it well."

"How do you know all this?"

Simon flicked at the screen. "Some of it is here and some of it I deduced from observation. Like I said, this is just what I think. I only have the ISP and electronic tracker, but I'm most certain the police will be able to confirm my theories."

Dr. Varela called the security company and it took them half an hour to arrive. Simon repeated his findings to them and they called the police. When two uniformed officers and a plain-clothes detective came, they conferred with Dr. Varela and the security officers for almost forty minutes and finally asked Simon to accompany them to the police station to take his statement and receive the flash drive with the evidence. The detective in charge of the case didn't speak English well and by that time Dr. Varela had already left, forcing Simon to wait until the interpreter arrived. If he left and came back the next morning, they'd probably make him wait for another detective and interpreter, or maybe even both. So Simon stayed until he'd signed all the forms, both in English and Portuguese.

It was after eleven at night when Simon finally returned to the apartment. He unlocked the door and dropped onto the sofa in the living room. If he had a blanket within reach, he might just spend the night there. But the small apartment was too cold, with the blinds still up in all the windows after having the rain hitting the glass all day. After a few minutes, Simon got up to draw them, then turned on the space heater. Was he hungry enough to make something before he slipped into bed? His stomach rumbled, answering for him.

After he warmed up a can of soup on the stovetop and ate it directly from the small pot, Simon sat in bed with his cell phone. He'd sent texts to Isabel throughout the day, but she hadn't replied to him.

He had to see her.

Before he changed his mind or got ready for bed, Simon called a taxi. He arrived at Isabel's building and rang the bell to her apartment. After three rings, the door opened and he went in. Hope rose in his chest. She was in and he was going to see her.

The door to her apartment was still locked when he got out of the elevator. Simon knocked on the metal surface.

"She left yesterday," a voice said behind him.

He turned. It was the neighbor young woman from the other apartment, with the door half open, wearing a man's shirt and nothing else. The top three buttons hung askew and Simon cast his eyes to the wall beside her.

"Excuse me?" he said.

"You looking for Isabel, yes?" Her English was heavily accented, but good enough for him to understand.

A man's voice sounded from inside the apartment. The girl turned her head and replied. Simon understood only two words, *Americano* and *professora*. American man and teacher lady. Him and Isabel.

The guy appeared at the door in his boxer shorts and hugged his girlfriend to his chest. *Frio* and *cama*, he said to her. Simon's neck heated and he looked away again. After almost four months in the country, his understanding of the Portuguese language was mediocre but good enough to let him know the guy was cold and asking his girlfriend to go back to bed with him. They were very uninhibited, for sure.

The young woman brushed off the boyfriend and brought her hands up in front of her. "Isabel have—" She made the shape of a small rectangle close to the ground. "Box, like dees."

"You mean a suitcase?" Simon kept his eyes on her face.

She nodded. "Yes, small suitcase. Yesterday."

So Isabel had left somewhere with a small suitcase. That was not good. He thanked them and left.

Within twenty minutes, Simon rang the bell at Cristina's apartment. He'd copied her cell number and address from the personnel files earlier, just in case, and he was now glad he'd done it. He hadn't planned to come this late, but this way he could look for Isabel first thing in the morning. Cristina buzzed him in and was waiting when he got out of the elevator in her building.

"Simon, what are you doing here? You do know it's close to midnight?" She was wrapped in a shawl and had pajama pants on.

"I know it's late, I'm sorry." He let out a breath. "I need to know where Isabel is."

Cristina shook her head. "She asked me not to tell you." She pulled on the knob and started closing the door on him.

Simon put a hand out in front of it. "Please. I really need to see her."

Cristina paused. "She said you couldn't be distracted from something you were doing at the academy."

"I'm finished with it, that's why I'm so late." He shifted in place. "I'm worried about her. She said—" He stopped himself. It was Amélie who'd told him she'd be away from a computer, not Isabel. He blew out a long breath.

Cristina bit her bottom lip. "Do you have a TV?"

He frowned. "What? No, I don't have a TV."

"So you didn't watch any TV this evening?" she asked.

"No, I was at the po—I was busy with something. What happened on TV?"

Cristina leaned against the door jamb. "But you have your laptop, right? Go home and look up the website for the PortugalHoje TV channel. They have several shows, but make sure you watch the one they had tonight at nine. Then tomorrow night you need to find a TV and set it to that same channel. Go to a café or something." She paused. "Better yet, go to the Tivoli Resort and watch TV there. The seven o'clock show. At night."

"The Tivoli Resort? Where is that?"

"It's across the bridge, in Almada. Be there early because it will be busy and crowded. You might have to wait three hours or more, but I'll text you where to go exactly when it's done."

"Cristina, what does all this have to do with Isabel?"

She tilted her head with a small smile. "Everything. If you like her half as much as I think you do, go and do as I told you." She closed the door.

Simon stood on the threshold for a moment. A website for a TV channel. The nine pm show. And tomorrow night at the Tivoli Resort, on the other side of Lisbon. A smile tugged his lips.

There could only be one reason why Isabel was linked to a TV show.

Chapter Twenty-two

To: ameliefaithfulfriend@mail.com
From: elliotbestpenpal@mail.com

Dear Amélie,

I haven't heard from you. I'm worried. Can you please let me know you're okay?

Yours,

Elliot

CHAPTER TWENTY-THREE

*I*sabel passed a hand across her forehead and rolled her shoulders back. She glanced up at the digital clock display on the wall behind the cameras. Eleven minutes left in this round. She looked at her station, making a mental note of what she'd done already and what was left to do.

Plating. That's what she needed.

She walked behind the counter to the metal shelving where all the kitchen gear and servingware were available and grabbed four rectangular plates. Thanks to the tour of the pantry on the first day, she knew where everything was placed. Remembering where all the items sat exactly was a different story. One of the camera men with the portable cameras followed her back but she ignored him.

That had been hard to get used to, all the cameras and lights, the microphones dangling over the stations, the cameramen running back and forth and the grips holding the electrical cords for them. Not to mention the make-up crew, the production team, and the program director. So many people on her heels and in her face all the time. But it was all coming to an end in less than an hour after the last dish was judged.

The pizzas cooled on the counter and Isabel cut them into triangles. She'd taken three of the most typical Portuguese dishes and given them a makeover as pizzas, inspired by the ones she'd made before on the night Simon had come for the first time. One square of each pizza for each judge, and the dipping sauces beside them: roasted pork, clams and parsley with lemon sauce; fried onions with salted cod and olives with an olive oil-infused yogurt sauce; and fruits of the sea pizza, a combination of lightly grilled shrimp, calamari, and sea scallops with a spicy tomato-cilantro sauce. Just enough heat to kick the other flavors.

Caldo Verde soup had lent its flavors to the salad appetizer and for dessert she'd planned a variation of the chocolate soufflés with a flan pudding sauce. Her menu drew inspiration from the traditional Portuguese flavors but she'd infused it with a light, modern twist. The feedback had been positive on the appetizer round, but the other contestants had received really good comments as well, and it was too early to figure out who might be ahead. Judges awarded points for originality, presentation, flavor, and an extra point for their favorites.

They couldn't be more different, Isabel and the other contestants: a retired construction manager named António who babysat his grandkids three times a week; Paulo, a university student majoring in computer science; and Marisol, a middle-aged woman who operated her own stall at the fish market. From what Isabel had observed in the elimination rounds, her most serious competitor was António. For a sixty-seven year-old man, he was still in great shape. Like her, he was an amateur, but being older gave him the advantage of more experience in the kitchen. Marisol and Paulo had enough passion, but they seemed less experienced and less comfortable.

The show had given Isabel and her opponents one hour for the entrée category and had allowed them some minimal preparation of the ingredients for each course. She'd made some mistakes, and so had the others, which was what the producers wanted for the show. Live broadcast conflict made for better reality TV than breezing through the whole thing without any problems. And they weren't professionals, after all. A lot was at stake, but she couldn't think about it, or the pressure might get to her. One task at a time would get her to the end, and that was all she wanted for now.

By the time the judges were done with the commentary on her entrée, Isabel welcomed the scheduled break for the sponsors' advertising, a blessed eight minutes to think of something else. Cristina came down the stairs to the edge of the stage and

Isabel joined her there with a water bottle in hand to sip from.

Cristina reached over the railing and hugged Isabel. "You're doing great. The judges loved your entrée, Isabel."

Isabel took another sip. "Do you think so? I was trying not to analyze their reactions."

Cristina touched her arm. "You're almost done now. What do you have planned for dessert?"

"A variation of the chocolate soufflés. Remember when I made those at the academy's kitchen?"

Cristina frowned. "I'm pretty sure I wasn't there. Those sound amazing and I would have remembered."

It was Simon who had been there, and he'd loved them. Isabel smiled at the memory. The five-minute warning buzzed and she blew out a long breath. "I need to go check my station and make sure I've got everything. Are you staying until the end?"

"Yes, of course. I wouldn't miss it."

Isabel drew in a breath. It was almost over now.

☙

Isabel turned as they called her name from each side, her smile in place while the camera flashed blinded her. More pictures by herself, pictures with the other contestants, pictures with the producers in front of the sponsors' wall.

One of the production assistants took her by the elbow. "This way, Isabel." Handshakes, hugs, congratulations—all from people she'd never met.

Second place. Isabel had won second place in the national amateur cook-off, a six-month paid internship at the Tivoli resort with the best chefs in the country.

She blinked again, half-expecting to wake up in her bed. Only the soreness in her muscles reminded her that the dream around her was very much the real deal, however strange it felt. The last segment on the show had flashed by in a blur, and Isabel had held on to her instincts and her memories of Avó Marta while she cooked and baked. She'd felt grandmother's presence beside her, as if cheering her on and reminding Isabel of all the little tips she'd always shared. The feeling in her chest expanded and brought a smile to her lips. Entering the amateur cook-off competition had been a hasty decision, wrought from a situation she couldn't control, but she was glad to have done it. Whatever happened going forward, Isabel had followed her dreams and Avó Marta would have been the first person to congratulate her. How she missed her.

Cristina had briefly hugged her before Isabel had been thrust in the media craziness. But now she couldn't see her anymore.

"Just a few more minutes, then we'll let you go get cleaned up," the assistant said.

Did she look that bad? She probably did, after so many hours cooking under the studio lights. She must look a fright. Isabel tucked her hair behind her ears, feeling the loose strands at the nape. She was sweaty and tired and ready to go to her hotel room for a long, long shower.

After a few minutes, all of the media attention was squarely on António, the first place winner, and Isabel took the second elevator to her room on the fifth floor. This is where they'd brought her on Wednesday, before the first part of the competition, and already it felt like a distant memory. So much had happened in the past three days, and so quickly too. In less than one week her life had taken another dramatic turn.

Isabel removed her shoes, then unbuttoned the white chef coat, her name embroidered over the show's logo.

A knock sounded at the door, and Isabel opened it to another assistant from the show.

He handed her a small black box with her smart phone and charging cord. "Don't forget to use the show's hashtags when you go on Twitter and Facebook."

She sat cross-legged on the bed and turned on the phone to find all the emails, texts, and voice mail messages she's missed since Wednesday morning. Too many to go through right now.

The phone rang in her hands and she answered Jacinta's call.

"Isabel, you were so fabulous," her cousin said.

"Thank you," Isabel replied. How many people who knew her had watched the show? How many live viewers in the country had the show tallied?

"How come you didn't mention you were going on national television?"

"It was a rather sudden decision. I didn't have the time to tell anyone." Almost no one.

"Knox and I are so happy for you, and so is the rest of the family. I'm sure you're tired so I'll let you go, but I'll call you soon so you can tell me all the details."

"You can count on that. Thanks for the call, Jacinta."

After hanging up, Isabel dialed Cristina's number. "Cristina, I'm sorry I missed you at the end of the competition."

"Isabel, are you back to the land of the plugged-in?"

The familiar humor brought a smile to her lips. "They just returned my phone and told me I can tweet with the show's hashtags." Isabel pulled another pillow closer and relaxed against the headboard.

"Did you come back to the city?" Cristina asked.

"I will tomorrow morning. I need to catch up on some sleep and I might as well enjoy the room here."

"Don't forget to go see Simon before you turn in."

Isabel sat up in bed. "Simon is here? Where?"

"He came over last night, very anxious to see you, so I told him to go to the hotel and be sure he didn't miss the show on TV," Cristina replied.

Isabel edged to the side of the bed. "He's probably left already. I'll call him tomorrow."

"He was there when I left. He and Mando hung out together in the hotel's bar to watch the competition on the flat screen." Cristina chuckled. "I wish I could have seen that."

Isabel shot up to her feet. "I'll talk to you later, Cristina. Bye."

Isabel flung her suitcase open and quickly changed into a pair of dark jeans, a T-shirt, and a cardigan. She found a pair of complimentary slippers by the bed instead of dealing with her boots, and let her hair down, finger-combing it with one hand and looking for the card key with the other. It would have to do. She didn't want to keep Simon waiting any longer.

The elevator ride to the lobby was on psychological time, each floor pinging by at lengthier intervals than it had going up. She crossed her arms to hold herself steady. What would she say to him?

The lobby was less crowded than before without the throng of journalists, but she didn't see Simon. Isabel checked all the corners and chairs and moved on to the bar, where she found him talking to the barman.

Simon jumped off the barstool and stopped in front of her, a wide smile on his face and his eyes warm and bright. How she'd missed that smile, his bracket dimples, and the familiar, beloved expression of his.

He took both her hands in his. "Isabel."

"Cristina just told me. I didn't know you were here."

"I tried to get hold of you." He leaned toward her. "I had to see you."

A few patrons held their phones up and Isabel faced the other way for a moment.

Simon turned to the barman, still holding one of her hands. "Pedro, is there a room we can use for some privacy?"

How long had he been there that he knew the barman by name?

"The breakfast room is not being used." The barman gestured to an adjoining room with a large decorated Christmas tree, its lights off.

Simon led Isabel by the hand to the far wall of the breakfast room, where a panoramic window opened up to reveal a view of Lisbon across the river. The rain and fog of a few days before had lifted and the city was dressed in twinkling lights flashing in colored bursts.

They sat in the upholstered bench that anchored the window.

"You saw the competition?"

"You were amazing, Isabel. I'm sure the judges had a hard time deciding who got first place."

Her cheeks heated and she brought a hand to her collar bone. "I'm glad I didn't win the first place. The publicity schedule will be crazy. And when they start building the restaurant, they'll be making a show out of that as well."

He raised an eyebrow. "Did you not enjoy being on TV?"

She shook her head. "I think I've had enough of that, although I still have to do some interviews and photo ops when I start the internship in January, but I asked for no special treatment." She looked out the window and took a breath. "I was furious on Monday when Dr. Varela told me about the embezzlement." Simon tugged her hand and she stopped to look at him.

"You're cleared." He smiled.

She straightened. "What?" Did she hear him right? "How?"

"I knew you hadn't done it. I just needed to prove it." Simon explained how he'd laid a trap and caught the culprit using a fake copy of her card. "Once I had that information, we turned it in to the authorities. They'll be picking up Carlos Macedo for questioning soon."

A sense of relief washed over her. "I worried a lot that first night, you know. How was I going to keep working at the academy with the chairman and the board suspecting me? It was just an impossible situation."

Simon looked away for a moment, then back at her. "I'm so sorry I couldn't tell you. Dr. Varela decided everyone was under suspicion and had me sign a confidentiality clause about it. He didn't want anyone to know I was hired to trace the person responsible for the embezzlement."

She nodded. "You were just doing your job. I'm sorry I didn't trust you."

"You don't have to worry about it anymore." Simon stroked a thumb across her knuckles. "But how did you decide to apply for the competition? I thought you didn't want to."

Isabel glanced down at their joined hands. "I did a lot of thinking, Simon." She raised her eyes to him. "In all honesty, the experience was somewhat unexpected. I've been adrift since Avó Marta's passing, avoiding the responsibilities that I have in my life."

Her grandmother's unexpected death had been a blow. "I'm not proud to say that I wavered after her passing. I held on to the last meaningful thing we'd done together, and I didn't want to lose that."

Simon shifted closer to her and nodded, his gaze unwavering. His quiet, confident expression encouraged her to go on.

"But on Monday, when everything seemed to be crashing down... It was something I had to go through, as hard as it was." She wiped a tear with the tips of her fingers. "And now this new path has opened up to me..." She sighed.

"One day at a time, Isabel." He touched her arm. "Sometimes we find out we are the strongest through the hardest experiences in life. It's when we discover we're not alone."

Isabel let out a steadying breath and straightened. "When are you going back to London?"

His expression relaxed. "The lease on the apartment doesn't expire until January 5th, so I have some time."

A ray of hope lit inside her. "Does this mean you're staying for Christmas?"

He smiled crookedly. "Unless you have any arguments against it?"

"None whatsoever." She smiled back.

As hard as Christmas was going to be without Avó Marta, Simon's presence would be a comfort to her. The closeness she'd felt at times with him—she hadn't imagined it. His eyes held a promise she recognized in herself, something that went beyond the attraction between them and was worth exploring further. Isabel wanted their friendship to deepen, very much so.

She sat straight. "I just remembered. I might have a friend come to visit for Christmas as well."

"Your friend is welcome to join us. I don't mind." Simon winked at her.

Would Simon feel the same if he knew Elliot was not a woman but a man?

"There's something I should tell you, Simon," she started.

A slight frown pulled at his eyebrows. "That sounds ominous. Should I be worried?"

She hurried to put him at ease. "No, there's nothing for you to be worried about. I don't want to hold anything back from you, or give the impression that I'm not being honest with you."

He reached for her hand and took her fingers in his. "Go on. I'm listening."

"This friend lives in London and we've been corresponding for almost fifteen years. We've never met in person but he's hinted he might be coming for Christmas." The possibility of finally meeting Elliot was one that brought both anxiety and excitement at the same time.

For a moment, he didn't say anything, just looked at her with an expression she wasn't able to read.

"Isabel, I don't want you to feel like you ever need to cut ties with your old life on my account. Your friends are in your life because you chose them to be there, and I respect that." Simon smiled and squeezed her fingers, and the gesture reassured her.

CHAPTER TWENTY-FOUR

To: elliotbestpenpal@mail.com
From: ameliefaithfulfriend@mail.com

Dear Elliot,
I'm sorry I didn't email you sooner. I couldn't get to a computer for a few days.

I did it! I was on a national cooking competition and I won second place. Thank you for your encouragement and believing in me. They meant so much to me.

Well, I'm going to be crazy and tell you that if you want to watch the competition, I'm not going to stop you. I attached a document with the link to it.

Or you can call me instead. Maybe it's time.

Your friend always,
Amélie

P.S.—My number is 01-615136.

༺❧༻

Simon pulled the scarf tightly around his neck. The rainy weather had cleared into bright blue skies and cold temperatures, and he was still trying to decide which he liked better.

When he turned the corner, Isabel's street came into view, her apartment building half-way down on the right side. He smiled. He'd come to cook and watch a movie with her on Saturday. On Sunday, they attended the book club together, and everyone had asked Isabel about the experience of cooking on a live television show. She'd happily recounted what went on behind the cameras and how crazy it was to broadcast a live show with so many people hovering around her while she tried to cook the best dishes of her life.

Afterward Simon had brought the ingredients to cook another of his family favorites when he was growing up—macaroni and cheese in the oven. Something Mom had made lots of times for him.

His relationship with Isabel had strengthened in the past few days, a little more each time they met. Simon had found himself giving her disguised clues pointing toward Elliot—silly stories about his university days, a conversation about his favorite books, and even a shopping list written in long hand.

Several times he'd seen the hesitation in her eyes, a question that didn't make it to her lips, a frowny smile he'd wanted to kiss away.

How he wanted to kiss her.

But he'd held back, wanting her to know everything first. When he arrived at the apartment on Sunday night, Amélie's email was sitting in his inbox.

It was like a confession, the last piece in the puzzle formed of all the parts that gave evidence to her true identity. The letter she'd been holding when they'd crashed on the street was only the beginning, and over time the feelings in his heart and the impressions in his mind had told him what he needed to know. Her declaration had only cemented all the little parts into a cohesive one. He'd run out of excuses. They were ready to meet in person.

Part of him was elated. He'd woken up early with the excitement barely contained in his chest. After all these years, he was meeting Amélie, his dearest, best friend. That he'd been able to find her in the first week of his new job was a miracle he'd never hoped for. As he'd gotten to know Isabel, the little doubts had slipped away one by one and, in the process, he'd fallen in love with her even more than he'd already been.

Now here he was at her door, about to take the biggest chance in his life.

Simon stared at the building's front door. It was Monday, in the middle of the day, and he hadn't thought of how to get past the locked door. Isabel was at the Tivoli, signing contracts and going over the schedule for the internship, and he'd told her that he had errands to run. Which he had—first shopping for Dad and mailing the package to London, then shopping for Isabel, including a postcard of a certain spot in Lisbon, a postcard he now held in his hand. The plan was to get it in her mailbox so she could see it when she arrived home in the evening, but first, he had to get inside the building.

After a few minutes of waiting, with nobody coming or going, he rang the bell to Isabel's next door neighbor. Maybe she kept odd hours and with some luck, she'd be home at lunch time and—

The intercom shrilled and a voice said something in Portuguese.

He bent down near the speaker. "It's Isabel's boyfriend." Well, he hoped to be, if everything went well. "Can you open the door, please?"

The buzzer clicked the door open and he went through. He approached the row of built-in mailboxes on the wall to the left and scanned the labels until he found the one he wanted—third floor, forward apartment.

He slid the postcard in.

෩

Dearest Amélie,
Indeed it's time.

Tomorrow at 1pm, at the place on the front of this postcard.

Yours,
Elliot

P.S.—Dress warmly.

CHAPTER TWENTY-FIVE

*I*sabel stepped off the eléctrico and glanced around the street. She took a breath and slipped her hand into her coat pocket.

Elliot's postcard.

He hadn't replied to her email, the one where she'd asked him to call her. Instead, she'd found the postcard when she got home last night. Elliot was in Lisbon, and she was about to meet him. She could hardly process the fact that he'd found her and had even dropped the card in person. Those would be questions for later.

Isabel barely slept the night before with thoughts of the meeting swirling in her mind. When she finally fell asleep, strange dreams came and went all night, dreams where everything went wrong, from not being able to find Elliot to being stood up in the rain to getting lost in all the places he wanted to meet her.

Between the restlessness and the anticipation, she rose from bed earlier than normal.

The English-style garden was quiet. A tourist couple stood by the ledge, taking pictures, and a group of three retired men sat on a bench facing the street, leaning over their canes and talking animatedly. Isabel walked in, descended the stairs, and chose a bench at the far end. The day had dawned cold and the sun shone high in a blue, cloudless sky. She'd dressed in layers but more than her coat, gloves, and scarf, the nervous energy inside flushed her cheeks and warmed her chest.

Elliot had chosen one of the city's belvederes to meet, one of her favorites, this one overlooking the eastern hills of Lisbon. It was a well-known spot in the city, sometimes crowded in the summer but today they would have privacy if they wished. And if it got too cold, there was a small café across the street. That the belvedere was located not too far from the academy and her apartment was only a coincidence, wasn't it? The questions kept piling in her mind and she told herself once more to hold off on overwhelming Elliot with too many of them. He hadn't even told her how long he was staying but surely there would be time for answers.

Her phone chimed.

Are you there yet?

It was a text from Simon.

Yes, I just got here, she replied.

She hadn't told Simon everything about Elliot, but he'd been accepting and understanding nonetheless. He knew where she was this morning and why, and that was enough for now.

See you soon, he texted.

She frowned. They hadn't made plans for him to come but maybe he wanted to meet Elliot.

Isabel took Elliot's postcard out again and read it. She'd memorized the words he'd written by now, but the sight of his slanted handwriting filled her heart with a warmth she didn't want to let go. Whatever happened, his friendship was still important to her.

"You're going to wear out that postcard, you know," a man's voice said. Simon sat down beside her and grinned.

She slipped the postcard back in her pocket. "Simon, what are you doing here?" It was hard to hide the surprise from her tone. He really had come.

"I changed my mind about this place. It's colder up here than I thought." He came closer and reached for her hand. "Are you cold?"

"It's always a little breezy in this garden." She stared at him. "I'm all right." Her pulse sped up, the questions mounting and tripping to come out, her mouth unable to voice them.

"It does have a nice view of the city, just like you said. I can see why it's one of your favorite places. And I bet the garden is beautiful when the wisteria is in bloom. Have you been here in the summer?"

Simon's hand was warm, even through her knit gloves. She kept staring at him. Upside-down feelings tumbled in her chest but his contact was firm and familiar, grounding her to the moment. The implications were too many to consider.

"Simon?" she asked again, her forehead wrinkling in a frown.

He shifted on the bench, turning to face her more fully, her hand still in his. A veil of resolution passed through his expression, his eyes softening. So much meaning in his gaze, so much tenderness.

Her heart tripped with a feeling she couldn't name. Isabel blinked and a tear rolled down her cheek. No, no tears to blur her vision, not when she needed to keep all her wits about her. She wiped it with a finger.

"What if I ask you to call me Elliot?" The gentleness in his voice completely undid her.

All the tears spilled at his words, flowing freely as her mind struggled with the knowledge her heart willingly took. "Elliot?" she whispered, touching a hand to her trembling mouth, searching his eyes for the truth, for the recognition that was long coming.

"It's me, Amélie," he said. "It's me, at last." He brushed away her tears, the warm skin of his fingers sending tingles through her cold cheeks.

Isabel watched him, the words still trapped inside her. How was this possible?

He drew both her hands into his. "Please say something, Isabel. Please tell me I haven't ruined everything."

She took a shaky breath. "When did you know? How did you find me?"

"That day when you crashed into my bike. I saw the letter you held, the one I'd sent as Elliot a few days before. I was so shocked I didn't know what to do, and I put it back in your pocket."

"What kept you from saying anything?"

"I wanted to make sure it was the right time. We didn't exactly start off on the right foot."

Isabel looked down, embarrassed by her behavior toward him. She'd been suspicious of his motives and trust hadn't come easy.

"But here," he touched his chest, "I never had any doubt, and I knew that first day when we met at the academy."

"I remember." Isabel nodded. She'd seen it in his eyes then, unable to recognize it for what it was, what it really meant.

"I've been trying to tell you." Simon bent his head to catch her eyes.

"Yes, I can see it now. The little hints you've been dropping. I thought I was going crazy at times." She shook her head, trying to hide a smile and failing.

Simon had the good sense to look abashed. "I had to make sure we were both ready for this." He lifted an arm around her shoulders and drew her closer to his side. "I didn't want to lose your friendship. Not yours and not Amélie's. You are so important and dear to me."

Isabel closed her eyes and hugged him back. His scent, the solidity of him, his arms anchoring her to this moment—a feeling of complete happiness in the embrace of the man she'd loved for so long.

For she loved him, didn't she? Even if she'd never before admitted it to herself, she loved him. She'd loved him as Elliot and she'd come to love Simon as well.

He passed a hand through her hair. "I almost bungled things, didn't I? When I asked you for that kiss."

Isabel drew back a little and tilted her head to look him in the eyes. "Simon, do you know you talk too much when you're nervous?"

His mouth curved into a lazy line. "Less talk, more action?"

She nodded, and his eyes darkened as he tipped his head in her direction. He raised a hand to her neck and settled the other on her waist. Their lips met.

Finally.

Relief and elation rose to mingle in her heart. The kiss was sweet at first, almost tentative. As the emotions they'd been holding in bloomed between them, it grew and it deepened, and Isabel finally understood the meaning of coming home to her best friend, the dearest friend of her heart.

Simon smiled against her lips, then trailed little kisses on her cheek and jaw. Her body trembled with pleasure, and she melted further into him.

He leaned over her shoulder and drew her hair aside, kissing her gently at the nape of her neck. "I've been dying to kiss this line of stars for a long time."

Isabel closed her eyes and held on to his arms, giving herself away to the sensations on her skin and in her heart.

Simon buried his face in her neck. He held her tightly against him and whispered in her ear. "Isabel, is it too soon to tell you how I truly feel about you?"

Was it? She drew back and touched the side of his face. Considering they'd just combined their first kiss with Elliot and Amélie's first meeting, she was ready to move forward.

"We've been writing each other for almost fifteen years, Simon. It's not too soon and I can't wait any longer."

He brought her closer and kissed her again. "I love you, Isabel," he said with a sigh. "I've loved you for so long. It's been always you and no one else."

"I love you too," she said against his lips.

His eyes widened and he swallowed hard, the Adam's apple bobbing in his throat. Then a smile tugged at the corners of his lips, deepening the lines on either side of his mouth.

They lost themselves into each other again and after a moment she pulled back and looked into his eyes. "How is this possible? I'm afraid I'm sleeping and I'll wake up to find this is only a dream."

He chuckled lightly. "I can assure you it's better than a dream because it's real. Very, very real."

What could be better than discovering that Elliot was Simon, the man she loved and who loved her in return?

He clasped her hand and stood, and she rose with him. The bracket dimple appeared in the lopsided smile she knew so well by now. "Come on, let's go somewhere warmer and with more people around or I might be tempted to keep kissing you for the rest of the day."

Isabel squeezed his hand. That was something she was beginning to understand only too well.

They ate lunch in a nearby restaurant, then took to the streets of Lisbon until the late afternoon, hand in hand. With Christmas only a few days away, the lights shimmered and the decorated windows in the downtown stores added to the festive atmosphere everywhere.

When darkness fell suddenly, they entered a grocery store and bought ingredients to cook a meal together at Isabel's apartment. At home, Isabel drew two aprons from the pantry and slipped one around Simon's neck, pulling him down for a kiss.

"We'll never get anything done this way," he said, smiling as he returned with more kisses.

"Are you complaining?"

"Never."

Reluctantly, she slipped from his embrace. She walked to the utensil drawer and handed him a paring knife to start peeling potatoes while she chopped onions beside him.

"I forgot to ask you how things went at the Tivoli," he said, glancing at her.

Isabel paused the chopping and turned to him. "I signed the contract. I'm starting the internship on January third." She smiled unable to contain the excitement. "I still can't believe it."

Simon put the knife down and pulled her in to brush a kiss on her forehead. "I'm so happy for you. I truly am."

Isabel leaned into him, amazed that it felt so right and so natural.

He placed the peeled potatoes in a bowl of water. "What about your position at the academy? Did you tell Dr. Varela yet?"

"I did, right after I was done at the Tivoli." She paused. "I asked for all the vacation time I have left and gave him my notice. He didn't like it, but I told him the internship is starting soon and I can't miss that."

Simon leaned against the counter. "Well, that would explain his frantic call just before lunch."

Isabel wiped her hands on the apron and stepped closer to him. "Just exactly how frantic was he?"

"Enough to beg me to stay and finish the school year."

Her eyes widened. "Truly?"

Simon stepped forward and rested his hands comfortably on her waist. "It turns out the academy is in need of an interim director until he can find a new, permanent one, and he thinks I'm the man for the job. Imagine that."

She matched his tone. "Imagine that indeed. But truth be told, you were trained very well for that position."

He pulled her closer. "Trained by the very best."

She placed her hands on his chest and her heart skipped a beat at the closeness between them. "So you'll be staying until June?"

"Until July. Dr. Varela wants me to post the marks and train the new director. That means I'll have over six months to look for a new job in Lisbon. Or even somewhere else." He raised an eyebrow. "What are your plans after the internship?"

"My contract with the Tivoli resort ends in July," she said. "And you'll be here until then," she repeated, happy with the news that Simon was staying in Lisbon through the beginning of summer.

He nodded, smiling. "You'll be an acclaimed chef with job offers pouring in from everywhere."

She chuckled. "Not likely." Then she sobered. "But I'm not really interested in taking any offers or going anywhere permanently until I find out what you'll be doing and where you'll go." It was true, and she didn't want to hold it back from him.

"What if we don't have to be apart, Isabel?"

She held her breath and stared at him. "Do you mean what I think you mean?"

Simon tucked her loose hair behind her ear. "Don't freak out on me, please. It's just an idea but I want you to think about it. When you're ready to discuss it, I'll be here."

"Okay." Isabel stepped into his embrace, the sound of his heart fast and loud against her ear, beating as wildly as her own. Here she was, in the arms of this incredible man who wanted to make plans for the future with her, and he was afraid she might not want the same. But she did, with everything in her power.

The confirmation came clearly to her mind, and the truth of that knowledge warmed her heart, freeing her of any inkling of a doubt.

"I think I'm ready now," she said.

His eyebrows knit in the adorable way she'd come to know. "You're ready now? You really are?"

She nodded, pulled on him and kissed him.

What was meant to be a quick kiss soon grew deeper as he responded with the same fervor she had.

"I love you, Isabel Antunes. I don't have a ring for you but I'm going to ask you anyway. Will you be my wife? Please?"

"I love you, Simon Ackerley. Yes, I will be your wife. Nothing will make me happier."

After another long kiss, she came up for air and smiled. "You're right. We're not getting much cooking done."

He raised an eyebrow, his expression both teasing and amused. "I happen to think we are getting a lot done."

Isabel laughed and kissed him again.

Epilogue

Six months later, on an evening in June

*S*imon grinned again. He'd woken with a smile on his face and he'd be smiling for a long time to come. In a few minutes, Isabel would exit the double doors and walk toward him to become his wife, making today the uncontested best day ever. For what could be better than getting married to his best friend and one true love?

When Isabel had told him how Lisbon had an old tradition of holding weddings in June, he'd readily agreed it was the best month for them to get married. She'd launched into plans with Cristina's help, and the weeks and months that followed had been the busiest in memory for both of them. Between Isabel's internship at the Tivoli and his position as the academy's director, they had worked all day every weekday, searched for an apartment on the weekends, and planned the wedding to take place eight days after the last day of school. A new, larger apartment had been found and decorated, and they'd moved their remaining belongings just a few days ago.

After waiting all this time, here he was now, standing under a flower-laden arbor that had been built for the occasion and placed in the academy's gardens. The weather had been hotter earlier but in the evening hour, and in the shade of old, familiar trees, the choice of venue was perfect for them.

Senhor Varela had been the one to propose they use the back gardens of the academy to hold the ceremony and festivities, surprising them both with the suggestion.

Simon looked around at the guests in the front rows. Armando was there, holding the seat next to him for Cristina who was Isabel's maid of honor. Isabel's cousin Jacinta and Knox, her American husband, had come from Porto to attend, along with Jacinta's parents. Almost all of the academy's staff and faculty were present, as well as some of Isabel's co-workers at the hotel.

Simon's dad, who had traveled from London, stood beside him in the role of best man.

"Are you nervous?"

Simon gave a quick shake of the head. "Just very excited to get married to her." Almost to the point of impatience.

"I still find it amazing you two connected after so many years of writing and not even knowing each other's names," Dad said. "Your mother would have been ecstatic to be here."

Simon took a deep breath and released it slowly. "She is here. I know she is."

Dad nodded quietly. "I think you're right."

When violin strains filled the air, everyone in attendance stood and turned around. The French doors opened and Cristina walked out first, but Simon's gaze focused on the woman behind her, the woman who had agreed to become his wife. His heart tripped.

Isabel lifted her eyes to him, a serene smile on her face and a purposeful stride in her steps. She wore a long, pearl-white dress that hugged her curves and waist, with short sleeves and lace inserts, and an elbow-length veil cascading down her back. The veil had belonged to her mother and the pearl comb pinning it to the crown of her head was an heirloom from her grandmother. Her father's ring hung around her neck from a simple gold cord.

As a surprise wedding gift, Isabel had conspired with his father and she'd given him a pair of cuff links made from his mother's favorite earrings, which he wore today. They had honored their loved ones in simple ways, simple objects that held meaning and made the day more special.

Simon's gift for her was a honeymoon trip to England, which he had somehow been able to keep from her knowledge. He could hardly wait to see her face when he gave her the plane tickets.

At last she made it to him. Her friend took her bouquet and Isabel stood facing him. Simon clasped her hands, the feeling of her skin adding an extra beat to his heart.

This was it.

Whatever luck or fortune or greater power in the universe, something had conspired on their behalf to bring them together. Serendipity may have had a hand in it, but it was divine design that kept them together.

"Here you are," he whispered. "All this time, I always knew I would find you."

Isabel's eyes shone bright. "You found me," she said in the same reverent tone.

∞

My darling Isabel,

On the one year anniversary of our wedding, how can I express into words the happiness in my heart?

All the hopes and dreams I had for us on our wedding day have been realized beyond my wildest expectations. The love we have for each other has grown more and more each day, and the friendship that bound us together for so many, many years has only strengthened our feelings and the togetherness between us. To say I'm excited for what lays ahead is an understatement, for what could be better than having you beside me for the rest of my life each and every day?

I look back fondly at the memories we've made in the past year—the honeymoon trip

to England in the late spring, visiting the
birthplaces of our favorite authors by day and
sleeping in each other's arms by night; our
summer evenings pedaling through Lisbon,
discovering anew all the places you'd told me
about so many times; our recharging weekends
in the fall, with Saturday mornings cooking
together and Sunday evenings of books and
movies, or sometimes none, losing ourselves
in kisses instead; and the long winter indoors,
each day at work looking forward to reuniting
with you again in the evening, knowing your
feelings for me run as deep as mine for you.

It's been a full, happy year, Isabel, not
entirely devoid of frustrations and setbacks as
we learned to share our lives in the same space
after living so many years alone—you don't like
how I forget to cap the tube of toothpaste and
I get annoyed when you use my razor to shave
your legs—but full of hope that we don't let the
minor disappointments and aggravations take
over the life we're building together.

If I haven't told you enough, I'll tell you
again—you are the love of my life.

I love you more today than I did a year ago,
knowing for sure how much more I'll love you
a year from now.

Your husband, who adores you,
Simon

Recipes

Spaguetti a la Bolognese

This is just one variation of this recipe. You may add different vegetables and herbs to make your own version. Don't be afraid to experiment with ingredients and flavors.

Prep time: 15 minutes
Cook time: 1-2 hours
Servings: 4-6

Ingredients:

1 tablespoon olive oil
1 large onion, chopped
2 cloves of garlic, minced
1 lb ground beef
1 can of chopped tomatoes
1 cup beef stock (more as needed for simmering)
1/2 cup tomato purée
1 package of fresh mushrooms, sliced (optional)
2 bay leaves
salt and pepper to taste
dried thyme and oregano to taste
freshly chopped parsley and grated Parmesan
   cheese (optional)

Directions:

In a shallow pan, brown the ground beef; season well with salt and pepper, and cook until meat is no longer pink. Use a wooden spoon to break up the meat into little pieces while it cooks. Drain and keep the beef on the side.

Add the oil to a large pan with a lid.

Add chopped onion to the oil and let it sweat. Add the garlic and cook until golden, be careful not to burn; it cooks quickly. Add the cooked ground beef, bay leaves, and beef stock.

Cook until liquid reduces slightly. Add in mushrooms, thyme and oregano.

Blend the tomato purée with a little bit of water, then add to pan along with the canned tomatoes, stir well then cover and cook on low for 1-2 hours.

As this dish slowly simmers you will need to add more liquid; use either beef stock or a little water. For a more authentic Portuguese flavor, substitute one cup of red cooking wine with the beef stock (the alcohol evaporates during cooking). Check the flavor and add salt and pepper if needed.

After one or two hours, turn off the heat and remove bay leaves. Stir well.

Garnish with freshly chopped parsley and grated Parmesan cheese to taste.

Serve with spaghetti and a tossed salad of dark greens seasoned with salt, olive oil, and vinegar.

❧

Chocolate Soufflés

This is an old Portuguese recipe that has been converted to American measurements.

Prep Time: 50 minutes
Baking Time: 18-20 minutes minutes
Servings: 4

Ingredients:

3.5 oz baking chocolate
1 oz of butter
8.5 fluid oz milk
2.5 oz granulated sugar
1 oz potato starch
1 teaspoon flour
3 egg yolks
5 egg whites
confectioners' sugar for dusting

Directions:

Liberally butter the insides of 4 individual soufflé dishes, or ramekins. Preheat the oven to 375° Fahrenheit.

In a small dish, dissolve the potato starch and flour in a little bit of cold milk and set aside.

In a sauce pan, add the sugar to the remaining milk and boil (allow to cool until just warm).

Melt the chocolate with one tablespoon of hot water, and add the warm milk mixture and the flour mixture to it. Cook on low heat and remove before it boils. Add the butter over the surface, shaved in little pieces.

Beat the egg whites into stiff peaks.

Add the egg yolks to the chocolate mix, one at a time. Fold in the egg whites carefully.

Pour in the individual dishes and place them on a baking sheet.

Bake for approximately 18-20 minutes, or until the tops have risen above the rim.

Remove from oven and transfer to serving plates. Garnish with confectioners' sugar and serve immediately.

Dear Reader,

Thank you so much for reading Simon and Isabel's story, *Always You*. I hope you've enjoyed reading it as much as I enjoyed writing it.

Please consider leaving a review on Amazon and Goodreads. This is the best way to support me as an author.

For news of upcoming books and promotions, join my readers club.

I love to hear from readers! You can email me at lucinda@lucindawhitney.com. Join my readers club on my website at lucindawhitney.com.

Thank you!

ACKNOWLEDGMENTS

When I had the idea to rewrite and update *One Small Chance*, I never expected to fall in love with Simon and Isabel again. Their new story, *Always You*, is more complete, with new content, extended scenes, and a swoony romantic epilogue. I dare you to not like it even more than the first version, if you ever read that one. I know I do.

I wish to acknowledge the help I've had in getting this book ready for publication: Heidi R, for her invaluable assistance in sorting out the old manuscript and for her timely suggestions; Julie C, for the amazing epilogue ideas (so many good ones, I had a hard time choosing); to my great proofreaders who caught the pesky typos, Natalya, Jillian, Mann, Marah, Bernadette, and Donna—you deserve the eagle eye award.

A special thank goes to Laura and Lindzee as partners/supporters/bouncers of ideas extraordinaire. It makes this journey worthwhile, ladies, to travel with you through the pothole-ridden roads of self-publishing. Ever onward!

And to you, dear reader, thank you for reading the stories of my heart! Thank you for your emails telling me how much you love my characters, for the positive reviews that give me the courage to go on, and for sticking with me every week when you open my emails. May I always have the ability to entertain you with my humble musings.

ABOUT THE AUTHOR

*L*ucinda Whitney was born and raised in Portugal, where she received a Master's degree from the University of Minho in Braga, in Portuguese/ English teaching.

She lives in northern Utah with her husband and four children. When she's not reading and writing, she can be found with a pair of knitting needles, or tending her herb garden.

She's the author of the *Romano Family* series and the multi-author series *Royal Secrets*. *Always You* is the first book in the *Falling For You* series.

Please visit her website at lucindawhitney.com for more information and news.